The Dog Who Ran with the Sleigh

Dorothy Bodoin

A Wings ePress, Inc.
Cosy Mystery Novel

Wings ePress, Inc.

Edited by: Jeanne Smith
Copy Edited by: Christie Kraemer
Executive Editor: Jeanne Smith
Cover Artist: Trisha FitzGerald-Jung

All rights reserved

Wings ePress Books
www.wingsepress.com

Copyright © 2020 by: Dorothy Bodoin
ISBN-13: 978-1-61309-581-2
ISBN-10: 1-61309-581-3

Published In the United States Of America

Wings ePress Inc.
3000 N. Rock Road
Newton, KS 67114

Dedication

In loving memory of my father, Nicholas Bodoin,
who gave me my love of books and dogs.
1893-1963

* * *

One

As I left the freeway, it began to snow, tiny glittering drops that landed on the windshield and promptly dissolved, like tears streaming down a glass surface.

How frustrating! According to the latest forecast, the snow was supposed to start after midnight, which would give me plenty of time for the drive home to Foxglove Corners after the play.

In an ideal world. Lately, my world was far from ideal.

Marston High School's Drama Club had chosen *A Christmas Carol* for their winter production. Principal Grimsley, in his never-ending obsession with making our school the best in the county, had decreed that every teacher must attend two student activities each semester. Ordinarily that wouldn't have presented a hardship unless a teacher lived a significant distance from Oakpoint.

As I did. The commute to and from Foxglove Corners, half on the freeway, half on dark country roads, was an hour in favorable conditions.

The snowflakes were larger now, the size of marbles. They didn't melt but clung to the window. I turned the windshield wipers to their highest speed, sending them flying back into the night air.

At least I knew the route, having driven this way twice a day for years. It shouldn't offer any surprises; and in less than a half hour, I would be turning into the driveway of the green Victorian farmhouse I shared with my husband Crane and our brood of eight collies.

You've driven alone at night and in snow before. This should be a piece of cake. So I told myself.

And watch out for leaping deer or any animal, for that matter, wild or domestic.

Unannounced, unexpected, a hulking barrier appeared through the falling snow. A large tree had fallen over the road, most likely downed by the high winds that frequently tore through Foxglove Corners. A gigantic trunk and a jumble of wood rose high above the surface. I couldn't possibly pass it.

Dear Lord! I might have run right into it.

Carefully I navigated a U-turn and drove back the way I'd come. About a mile to the west was another road I could take that would allow me to bypass the fallen tree and eventually lead back to this one. And I could only hope there wouldn't be any more obstacles ahead.

Something told me it was going to be a long drive home. I didn't listen; I had already realized it.

~ * ~

The snow lay heavily on the new road, untraveled and untrampled. I was puzzled. Why so thick a layer? The snow had started only a little while ago. It lay just as heavily on the woods that bordered the road, sticking to bare branches. Well, no mystery. Obviously, the storm had started earlier in this section of the county.

I wasn't happy at the delay. In fact, I was growing more nervous by the minute, and I was hungry. I wanted dinner and the comforts of home. Crane, the gun he wore as deputy sheriff safely locked in its special cabinet, and the collies with their warm fur and playful antics. Home.

Soon now. I drove on, hoping to find the road or by-road that would take me in the right direction. Instead, I found myself following a curve, then another one. Fate seemed determined to play havoc with my sense of direction.

I didn't dare increase my speed on the slippery road. On the right, the land sloped down to a low basin. From the car, I could barely make out the tops of trees through swirling snow. It would be a long way to fall.

Best not to think about that, to concentrate on what lay ahead in the meager illumination cast by the Ford's bright lights.

A happy clanging sound insinuated itself into my thoughts. Sleigh bells? They rode the air like high, silvery entities, each one separate and distinct.

The next moment a sleigh materialized out of the snow and into clear view. It moved with the ringing of the bells and the laughter of the four riders.

I saw it all in a brief glimpse: evergreen roping wrapped around the honey-brown sides of the sleigh; the pair of dark prancing horses; the young riders, two men and two women. And the dog, who ran ahead of the sleigh as if to guide it. The animal was a collie, a pretty Lassie lookalike, with a full white collar and white blaze.

I saw it all. All coming toward me!

The sleigh was going to crash into me! Didn't any of the people inside see the car in their path? Their collective gaze appeared to be fixed on the white expanse spread out behind me. I and my car might have been invisible.

Instinctively, I stepped hard on the brakes, lost the road, and slid down the incline as if airborne.

~ * ~

It was over in seconds, a dizzying downward flight, crushing through trees, crashing into a stand of evergreens. Jolting to a stop. Earthbound.

My head slammed into something. The steering wheel. Instant pain spread from my left temple down to my hip.

Pain meant the ability to feel; feeling meant that I was alive.

So high above me they might have come from the sky, I heard the sleigh bells ringing. They were still loud but growing fainter every second.

For an instant, white-hot anger overrode the pain. How could the people in the sleigh have continued on their merry way, leaving me dead, for all they knew? Whoever heard of a hit-and-run sleigh?

Don't worry about that now.

I forced myself to move and found that I could.

Now what?

The car? My trusty Ford Focus?

Its air bags had protected me, but now I had to move around them.

The crash had crumpled its left side. The driver's side window had a long crack but thankfully, hadn't shattered. I tried to coax the engine to life. It was no use.

That meant I'd have no heat—for as long as it would take me to extricate myself from the situation.

If that were possible.

I crawled over the front seat, every part of my body protesting the exertion, and exited awkwardly through the passenger's side. Standing knee deep in snow, I looked up into a wall of moving white that hid the road from my view. No matter. I could never climb back up.

The evergreens had broken my fall at the halfway point of the incline. I could have fallen farther yet. Could be dead.

I couldn't stop thinking about my narrow escape.

The air was thick with the rich scent of balsam, a spicy, evocative fragrance I'd always loved. But tonight the balsam smell was too intense. Nauseating even.

And I was so cold, shivering in the frigid temperature and in the aftermath of the shock.

I could be dead at the bottom of the incline. Feeling nothing.

Luckily, I had dressed warmly for the play, with a black wool boot skirt, the requisite high boots to go with it, and a turtleneck under my purple parka. I had leather gloves in the car, and a blanket in the trunk for my work with the Collie Rescue League.

So I wouldn't freeze. Yet.

I brushed the stinging snow away from my face and remembered my cell phone. I knew it was in my purse because I had turned it off so it wouldn't ring during the play. Thank heaven for modern inventions and caring husbands. All I had to do was call Crane.

As for my car, I'd have to leave it where it had come to rest on the incline. Even if it had started, I could hardly drive uphill.

I'd be home soon. Not the way I'd envisioned it, but home, nonetheless. Safe with Crane and my collies, I'd leave this terrible night behind forever.

Two

Once Crane arrived, I knew everything would be all right. The lights of his Jeep created a welcome oasis in the snowy night. He stood in its center for a moment, tall and commanding and dependable. Just what I needed after my harrowing experience.

He strode down the incline seemingly with no effort, as if it were level ground, and climbed to the top again, taking me with him. My handsome, blond knight in a sheepskin jacket and gun belt. Why, I wondered, wasn't his gun locked in its special cabinet? Did he expect trouble?

I was about to ask him when he said, "Are you sure you're okay, honey?"

His frosty gray eyes were cold, but his voice with its hint of a Southern accent was warm. The temperature around us seemed to rise.

When I'd talked to him earlier, I'd assured him that I was unhurt but had to admit that I didn't know what road I'd been traveling on when misfortune struck.

"I'll find it," he said. "Close to the freeway exit—right? You get back in the car and sit tight."

That was something I could happily do.

Now he was here. We stood together on the road which turned out to have quite a civilized name: Windemere.

I took one last look at my car in its unyielding embrace of evergreens. The trees had likely saved my life, preventing me from falling all the way down to the incline's basin. Crane promised to arrange for it to be towed. All I had to do was settle myself in the Jeep. I grabbed the door's handle, not surprised to find it was encrusted with ice.

Crane laid his hand heavily down on top of mine. "Wait, Jennet."

"For what?"

"Something's wrong here."

"Yes, very wrong. That's why I called you."

"Look at the ground," he said. "The snow is pretty churned up, but I can tell where you skidded off the road."

I did as he said, shuddering at the memory. "I never, ever want to go through anything like that again."

"You won't, if I have anything to say about it. "He moved his hand up to my shoulder. "The sleigh that ran you off the road...I don't see any tracks."

With those words, with that grim observation, he effectively erased the last hours of my life, my perception of them, that is.

"They have to be there," I said. "There was the horse-drawn sleigh, and a dog running in front of it. Oh, I know. The tracks are snowed over."

"Snow didn't cover *your* tire tracks."

I forced myself to look, to see the skid marks. The broken brush that had the misfortune to grow at the top of the incline. Saplings crushed as the car plowed through them.

Something else was wrong.

There didn't appear to be as much snow as there had been before when I'd been driving. Neither on the road, nor in the surrounding woods.

How could that be?

My confusion boiled over into anger. I wanted to challenge somebody. Not Crane. Never Crane. He was eminently objective and thorough. Always so thorough. If only I could summon one of the men in the sleigh, one of the hit-and-run drivers.

But...If Crane didn't see evidence that a large old-fashioned sleigh had forced me off the road, then the sleigh was a fiction.

Now *that* was wrong. I *had* seen the sleigh, and the four revelers, and the horses—and the Lassie dog. I couldn't possibly be mistaken about the collie. They were my reality, and I wasn't about to give them up. After all, why should I?

"We'll figure it out," Crane said.

I accepted his help stepping up to the Jeep, biting my lips to keep from crying out as the pain in my head and side soared way beyond ten.

"I just want to go home," I said.

"We'll get there, but first I'm taking you to Emergency."

"No," I said. "I'm hurting, yes, but nothing's broken. I can move, and I don't have a concussion, if that's what you're thinking."

"We're going to the hospital," he told me. "It's non-negotiable."

I knew better than to argue with him. First, the accident had drained the last of my energy. Then in a disagreement such as this, especially one that concerned my well-being, Crane almost always emerged the winner. Besides, he was driving. As for myself, I didn't think I'd want to get behind the wheel of a car for a long time.

Maybe not until spring.

~ * ~

It came as no surprise that the doctors in the Emergency Room found me bruised and battered but otherwise in good shape. They told me to take an over-the-counter pain medication and wait for my body to heal. What a waste. All we had accomplished was a further delay in reaching home. It felt as if an entire night had passed since I left Marston's auditorium.

But we were home now, turning onto Jonquil Lane, guided by the yellow Victorian across the lane with lights in every window. Only one lamp burned in our front window, but all the dogs were barking their traditional welcome.

Ever the Southern gentleman, Crane helped me down from the Jeep. "I brought home a pizza for us," he said. "It's keeping warm in the oven."

"I *am* hungry," I said. "And thirsty, too. I could drink a whole pot of tea."

He pushed open the side door and our collie pack converged on us, yipping, wagging their tails, nudging us with long noses, vying for attention.

Pay attention to me. No, me. Me!

When people asked why we had so many collies, Crane usually answered with his own brand of humor, "We've officially become a kennel."

I gave a more serious explanation. "Because we kept our rescues." I went on to explain that Halley—at this point I usually touched her head lightly—was the only dog I had actually purchased. The others began lives somewhere else under circumstances that, in most cases, remained a mystery.

Contentment wrapped its arms around me as I surveyed my collies, and I felt instantly better.

Halley and Candy, the two tricolor girls, were prancing around our feet, each one determined to enjoy the first pats. Our timid blue merle, Sky, had detached herself from the others and taken refuge under the dining room table. Raven, the rare bi-black, joined her, while Gemmy and Star, both sables like Lassie, were patiently waiting to be noticed. Misty, my tri-headed white, had slipped past us and was sitting at the door.

Who did I miss? Ah, yes, Velvet, our third tri and the last to join our household.

"Velvet?" She bounded out of the living room with her new toy, a green dinosaur.

We were all accounted for.

"Back," Crane ordered. "Let Jennet sit down."

They fell back, always quicker to obey Crane than me, and I sank into one of the oak chairs. Crane had already set the table and put the water on to boil for tea while I'd been counting collies. The kitchen smelled heavenly—of pizza. The dogs found places as close to the table as possible.

Unable to sit still, I found my new Christmas teapot, decorated with holly and ivy, and filled it with loose Red Rose.

"That's all I want," I said. "Tea and pizza."

He brought the pizza out of the oven and issued another warning to the dogs to keep their distance. They had obeyed his previous commands, but Candy and Misty were inching imperceptibly closer to us, convinced that we wouldn't notice.

"You already ate," he told them.

This they ignored. When we had pizza for dinner, they feasted on leftover crust.

Food, especially food eaten in my own kitchen, had a marvelous restorative effect. I still had pain, and dreaded looking in the mirror for fear of what I'd see, but my initial shock at not finding sleigh tracks where they should be had faded slightly.

I took my first bite of pizza. Mushroom, cheese, pepperoni—better by far than any pain killer.

"I think I know what may have happened tonight," I said.

Three

"It must have been an apparition," I said. "That would explain why there were no sleigh tracks in the snow."

Crane paused, a piece of pizza halfway to his mouth. "All of it?"

"I'd say so."

"A multi-ghost apparition with sound effects? Isn't that unusual?"

"Yes, in my experience."

I frowned, suddenly not so sure. Since coming to Foxglove Corners, I'd seen more than one ghost, all single entities. Like the skater who had glided gracefully across the frozen water of Sunset Lake until the ice broke, sending her to her grave. Or the traveler who haunted the halls of the Spirit Lamp Inn.

Never had a sleigh filled with people, their horses and dog, materialized in front of me on a road, causing a near-fatal accident. A new thought dropped into my mind.

Never had denizens from the other world placed me in harm's way by their actions.

I let my pizza cool for a moment, drank my tea, and sent my thoughts back to that brief encounter, before I realized that the sleigh was going to run me down. Before I'd panicked and slammed on the brakes.

Details I didn't remember noticing worked their way into my mind. Crane listened intently while I described them.

"I saw four people, two men and two women. They were young, maybe in their early twenties. One of the women had dark hair and wore a red coat. The other was a blonde; her head was covered with a bright green scarf. One of the men was very handsome. The other... Well, he didn't stand out.

"The sleigh was trimmed with greens and red ribbon, and the horses were decorated, too. The sleigh bells were loud...deafening. I heard them ringing before and after I saw the sleigh. No one was looking at me. They appeared to be in high spirits."

"Dashing through the snow?" Crane asked.

"Exactly. They were focused on the road or the scenery. It was spectacular...woods covered with fresh snow."

"That's a lot to notice in...What? One or two seconds?"

"I guess so, but that's what I saw. If I were an artist, I'd draw you a picture. It was the kind of scene you see on any Christmas card."

"Is there any chance they could be real people—I mean, live people—out for an old-fashioned sleigh ride, the kind they offer at Five Oak Farm?"

"They didn't belong to our time," I said. "I could tell. Then, if they were actual people, wouldn't they show some awareness of what was about to happen and rein in the horses?"

He couldn't argue with that.

"Well, if you'd been on Huron Court, you could have driven into the past," he said, referencing that road where the seasons and time changed, hurling unwary travelers into another century.

"Maybe Huron Court isn't the only time-traveling road in Foxglove Corners. But I think it was an apparition I saw."

A stray detail nagged at me. When Crane arrived, it was snowing but not enough to account for the accumulation on Windemere Road and the surrounding area. On our drive back, there was less snow. It was as if a plow had driven through, but that would never happen on a country road with a storm in progress. How could I explain that?

I couldn't. Neither could I understand how all of the details I'd just shared with Crane, like the color of a scarf, had imprinted themselves indelibly on my mind in so short a time.

"After the car crashed, I heard sleigh bells," I said. "They were moving away from me."

I could almost hear them now, full and clear in the frosty night.

"Whatever happened, it's over," Crane said. "You lost control of your car on a slippery road. It happens. That's all anyone has to know."

"Right."

I slid another piece of pizza onto my plate. Our friend, Lieutenant Mac Dalby of the Foxglove Corners Police Department, was a master of condescension. He would no doubt tell me the sleigh was a figment of my imagination, after which he would make some unflattering comment about women drivers.

I hoped he wouldn't find out.

The only people I would confide in were my friends. They would believe me. As Crane did. As I thought he did.

Of course he did.

"You can sleep in tomorrow and Sunday," Crane said. "I'll take care of the dogs and make my own breakfast."

How could I have forgotten the weekend? I'd been dreading the thought of facing my classes with a bruised face. I still hadn't looked in a mirror. Now I could postpone the inevitable for two more days.

Just tell them the truth, I thought. *You had an accident on the way home from the play.*

That should garner some sympathy and perhaps a flippant remark or two from kids who hadn't learned the fine art of discretion.

"By Monday I'll be back to normal," I said.

He smiled. "You will. You dodged another bullet, honey."

I could only hope that I'd seen the last of the sleigh from yesteryear, that it was a one-time manifestation, along with the horses that pulled it, and the dog that ran in front of it.

~ * ~

As soon as we finished dinner and the dogs went out for the last time, Crane and I went to bed. As usual, Halley and Misty settled themselves in the doorway to guard against nighttime intruders. Exhausted from a day that had been too eventful, I fell asleep as soon as I lay my head on the pillow.

But I couldn't escape the evening's trauma, not even in sleep. A sleigh with gleaming wood and a mesmerizing glow glided through my dreams. It moved without horses, but the Lassie collie ran silently alongside it. Her collar was made of balsam boughs and trailing red ribbon.

The sleigh was empty. The four revelers from the apparition were gone, but the bells rang. The sound was too loud. Unpleasant. Unreal.

I stood in the sleigh's path wearing only a long flannel nightgown, wanting to move, but unlike the sleigh, unable to. I watched in horror, knowing that the sleigh was going to run into me. Knowing I could do nothing to stop it.

In the last moment of my life, I woke. *Oh, thank heavens!*

I turned painfully. Every part of my body ached, reminding me of its recent abuse. Still, I forced myself to swing out of bed and walk across the room to the window.

The snow had stopped, leaving a winter wonderland in its wake. Light from the sky and the front window of the yellow Victorian across the Jonquil Lane filled the landscape with glitter. Everything in my view was so beautiful I felt like crying.

It's going to be all right, I told myself.

Four

The weekend passed in a blur of inactivity. Crane had my car towed. I stayed home and read but managed to take care of the dogs and cook dinner for us on Saturday.

On Sunday Camille, having heard about my accident from Crane, brought over a roasted chicken and an apple pie, together with a box of pineapple drop cookies. As we sampled the cookies over tea, she asked, "Are you in much pain?"

"Some. Did Crane tell you about the sleigh?"

"What sleigh?"

Ah, he'd kept my secret, realizing it was my story to tell. So I told it.

"Oh, my dear," she said when I'd finished. "Not again."

"Well, we *do* live in Foxglove Corners, Home of the Strange," I pointed out.

"But not everyone sees ghosts, and it's Christmastime. Aren't witches and other evil beings supposed to lose their power at this time of year?"

"According to Shakespeare, yes, but that's only on Christmas Day. Besides, there was nothing evil about the sleigh. The people, the ghosts, I mean, looked happy."

"But they ran you off the road."

"Yes. As if they didn't see me."

"Be careful," she said. "If you see a sleigh bearing down on you, go the other way."

Which was what I had done.

~ * ~

After Camille left, the day dragged. Time had never moved more slowly, but Monday came too soon.

In the morning, I dressed with the season in mind, choosing a red maxi dress, then adding my crystal snowflake pendant, and an extra layer of powder. It didn't help, but I decided I looked more pathetic than horrible. With a teenager's brutal honesty, my students would let me know whether or not my makeup was effective.

Crane left for his patrol of the Foxglove Corners roads and by-roads. I packed a lunch and waited for Leonora, my friend and fellow English teacher at Marston. We took turns driving to Oakpoint. This was my week, but Leonora had promised to take me anywhere I wanted to go until my car was repaired.

Like the young woman from the sleigh, she wore a long green scarf. With a matching knitted hat over her golden blonde hair she looked bright and cheerful for the early hour and pretty as always.

I dropped my books in the back seat and turned to face her.

"Oh, Jennet, it looks so bad. You poor thing."

She knew about my accident but not about the sleigh. I told my story again, adding the recently-remembered details.

We were on the same road that I had been forced to leave on Friday night. It had been plowed, and although I thought I knew every inch of it, I couldn't tell where the tree had fallen. Had it been removed already?

"Were you on Huron Court when this happened?" Leonora asked.

"Nowhere near it."

"I don't know what to think. It's so weird. Could you have imagined it?"

"No."

"I mean, this is such a stressful time of year. I feel like I'm being pulled in different directions."

"I'm not stressed," I said.

"Now that Jake and I are married, I have twice as many cards to write, and I have to bake and decorate and shop for presents. It's never-ending, but I'm loving every minute. I want our Christmas to be perfect," she added.

As she paused to take a breath, I repeated, "I'm not stressed."

"You should be, with company coming."

Crane's father, his aunt Becky and brother, Clem, were driving up from Tennessee to spend the holidays with us. His Uncle Gilbert would have been a fourth guest, but a few years ago he had fallen in love with Camille. Now happily married, Gilbert and Camille lived in the yellow Victorian across the lane.

We also expected Crane's cousin, Suanna, who usually spent Christmas with the Fergusons.

I wasn't sure who was going to stay with us but assumed it would be Crane's aunt. Then, of course, my sister, Julia, planned to spend her vacation in Foxglove Corners.

"I'm going to enjoy every part of Christmas," I said. "I refuse to let stress spoil things."

Leonora entered the freeway, and we were both happy to find it was plowed and traffic was light for a Monday morning. "I should have gone to the play with you," she said. "Then you wouldn't have been on the road alone."

That had been our plan, but Leonora had backed out at the last minute, feeling like she was coming down with another cold.

"It wouldn't have made any difference," I said. "Anyway, I could have spent the night in a hotel. I just wanted to get home."

"I understand." Abruptly, she turned the focus on her own situation. "Now, I've run out of activities to chaperone. Grimsley's going to be upset with me."

"You can't help being sick with all the germs floating around our classrooms. Tell Grimsley you'll chaperone three events next semester."

"I'll do it, and I won't wait until May."

I sat back and looked out the window. The scenery was uninspired. Fewer woods, more houses, less snow. As we neared the Oakpoint exit, I noticed a mere dusting of snow on the rooftops. Oakpoint had been spared the three inches that had fallen to the north.

"Our classes are going to be wild today," Leonora said.

"Definitely."

Nothing affects students of any age more than an impending holiday. Especially Christmas.

Count the days until winter recess, I thought and said, "I'm ready for them."

~ * ~

I was well prepared for the day's lessons. On paper. I hadn't factored in their curiosity about my battered appearance. The questions began in my first class with Randy's impertinent comment. "Wow, Mrs. Ferguson! Did you run into a door?"

"What does the other guy look like?" asked Connie to a chorus of giggles.

I gave my set speech. "I lost control of my car on the way home from the play."

Anyone would think that would satisfy them. But they wanted to know exactly how I'd lost control, as it hadn't been snowing in Oakpoint.

I pointed out that weather could vary in different parts of Michigan, adding, "I must have hit an icy patch. It happened so fast I really can't remember. Can we get back to our story?"

We were reading an abridged version of Dickens' novelette, *The Chimes*. My own real-life ghost story had more action, but I could never tell them about it.

Reluctantly, they began the day's reading.

The same inquisition happened in every class, although my English Literature students, mostly seniors, had slightly more tact.

I hadn't seen Principal Grimsley yet and was happy not to have to respond to his remarks. Although I could have taken the opportunity to remind him of the perils of driving home alone after an evening activity.

Forcing back a rueful smile, I could almost hear him tell me to move closer to the school, then, or find another position.

During our short lunch period, Leonora and I ate in her classroom or mine, dining on sandwiches, fruit, and cookies from home. She wanted to build a case for her theory that I'd conjured a sleigh out of holiday stress. I didn't understand why she was so quick to dismiss my apparition, as she was no stranger to the ghosts of Foxglove Corners.

Finally she capitulated. "Okay, say you saw a sleigh with four people in it."

"Four ghosts. And two horses and a dog."

"A collie, of course. You always see collies. What were the ghosts doing?"

"Going for a holiday ride in the snow. Obviously. The dog was running in front of the sleigh."

"They weren't aware of you?"

"They didn't act like it. They just kept coming."

"What about the animal ghosts? The horses and the dog?"

"Like the people, they didn't see me."

Safe in my classroom, removed in time and space from the terrifying situation, I felt the icy cold grip of fear again. The sleigh was going to run over me!

"I've been thinking," Leonora said. "If all of it was an apparition, they would have driven right through you. Like fog. You didn't have to try to get out of their way. And if you hadn't slammed on the brakes, you wouldn't have driven off the road."

"That's true, but I didn't think. I just reacted."

Even if what Leonora said was true—and it sounded reasonable—I wouldn't have had the nerve to keep driving in the sleigh's path. But then, why speculate on what might have been? It happened the way it was meant to.

I'd rather think about the ghosts themselves, the four revelers I'd seen so clearly. They'd been alive once, possibly living in Foxglove

Corners. Now that I knew I was going to be all right, and my car would soon be drivable again, I wanted to know more about them. For instance, why were they haunting Windemere Road?

Perhaps the key to understanding the apparition was knowing the histories of the four people who were apparently spending their afterlives together on a never-ending sleigh ride.

Five

On the way home from school, Leonora and I veered from our usual route. We both wanted to see where my car had gone hurling down the incline.

"I'd like to see a Christmas apparition, too," Leonora said. "You described it so beautifully."

She'd come a long way from believing that I'd conjured the sleigh and its riders out of thin air and stress.

"I've learned that ghosts don't come when called," I said. "They appear in their own good time and when you least expect them."

"I can hope. Look at all the ghost stories associated with Christmas."

There were no other cars on the road at present, no sign of wildlife, nothing but curves and woods. Last week's detour couldn't have taken me to a more isolated place.

"The ghosts must be in hiding today," Leonora said.

"Letting the horses rest on another plane," I added.

Fortunately, no one could hear our conversation. Plain talk about the supernatural required privacy, even in Foxglove Corners, this hotbed of psychic activity.

We passed one curve, then another. My heartbeat quickened. "It's close," I said. "Slow down. Right here."

She brought the car to a stop at the side of the road. As no new snow had fallen over the weekend, the disturbance in the incline where the car had crushed saplings on its descent was frighteningly clear, only a little drifted over from the wind.

"Oh, my gosh," Leonora said. "You could have been killed."

"The balsam trees saved my life. If they hadn't been there to stop the car…" I didn't finish. We both knew what might have happened.

I looked away, back to the road, and flashes of memory assailed me. I could almost see the sleigh again, a burst of red and green against pure white and the glossy darkness of wood. And did I hear sleigh bells? No…That sound was the wind blowing.

But a dog was barking in the distance. The dog from the sleigh?

Not likely. Except for the bells, the apparition had been silent. Horses' hoofbeats, merry laughter, all without sound.

"Do you hear that?" I asked Leonora.

"The dog barking? Yes. I hope the poor creature has a nice warm home to go to." She turned the heat up a notch. "Well, I've seen enough, Jennet. If the sleigh was on the move, it'll probably appear next in another location. Who knows where that will be?"

"If it ever comes back."

I'll admit I was conflicted. At first, I'd hoped never to see the phantom sleigh again. Now I wished it would reappear, somewhere, anywhere, as long as it passed me by at a safe distance.

Well, as I'd told Leonora, whether I saw the apparition again was beyond my control. Meanwhile, time was passing.

"Do you want to pick up dinner at Clovers?" she asked, again demonstrating that she was amenable to change. When she'd first married Jake, she'd balked at serving him restaurant meals. I'd convinced her that on days like this, when we were running late, it only made sense.

Besides, Clovers wasn't just any restaurant. The owner, Mary Jeanne, specialized in home-cooked comfort food and the best desserts in the county. My friend, and sometime partner in detection, Annica, worked there as a waitress to pay for her tuition and books at the university. I knew her schedule and didn't expect to see her today.

"I'd love to," I said.

"Then we'll backtrack. I'm not brave enough to make a U-turn on this narrow road."

"Heavens, no." I glanced out the window and shuddered. One tumble halfway to the earth's core was enough for a lifetime.

"Go straight," I said. "This road has to end sometime."

~ * ~

We bought roast turkey dinners at Clovers. I added a salad and banana-nut bread, and voila! dinner was served. The evening was quiet, exactly what I needed after a difficult day at school. Crane read the *Banner*, I started reading a new Gothic novel, and Misty and our new addition, Velvet, entertained us with a mock battle that looked ferocious but was only collies at play.

One day down.

I was eager to feel a hundred percent better and to use less makeup. Also, I wanted my car back. While relying on Leonora and Crane, I'd reconsidered my earlier reluctance to drive. After all, I knew how to handle a car on winter roads. As long as there were no sleighs around to collide with me.

In the meantime, I could begin readying the house for the holiday, taking little steps like unpacking ornaments and candles.

Days passed, and suddenly, it was Friday again. I came straight home after school, put a roast in the oven, and began decorating the mantle with silver Christmas trees, glitter-coated reindeer, and my white Father Christmas figure. Everything had to be perfectly placed.

A car door slamming pulled me from my concentration. The collies came together from their various resting places and rushed to the vestibule, breaking the silence of the house.

I wasn't expecting company, but one person never gave prior notice of his arrival. His vintage white Plymouth Belvedere with its fanciful green fins occupied the place where my Ford Focus should be. He was lifting bags out of the trunk.

"Yes, it's Brent," I told the collies. "And yes, he has something for you. Back!"

They went forward, eight collie bodies pressing against wood. One day they were going to break the door. I opened it, and they would have spilled out into the evening if Brent hadn't waved the bags under their collective noses.

Snowflakes sparkled on his dark red hair and forest green jacket, adding a touch of seasonal glitter to his rugged appearance. He pulled off his gloves, stamped snow from his boots on the doormat, and greeted each collie by name while I hung his jacket. Suddenly, the house radiated with energy. I realized how much I'd missed company this past week.

"I have treats from Pluto's Gourmet Pet Shop," he said, "and flowers for you, Jennet."

A sweet, spicy scent of carnations wafted into the air as he freed the bouquet from its wrappings. They were red and white, mixed with holly berries and fern. Perfect for my Christmas display.

"Ah, thank you," I said. "I'll go put them in water."

Brent Fowler was Foxglove Corner's pride and its best-kept secret. Entrepreneur, perennial bachelor, and fox hunter, Brent was a cross between Lord of the Manor and Robin Hood. Women adored him. Men respected him. I considered him one of our best friends. He had helped extricate me from many a perilous situation.

"Have a seat," I said. "Where have you been keeping yourself?"

"Out and about. Mostly about."

Strangely, he didn't look his usual jovial self.

"I just heard you were almost killed last week," he said. "I ran into the sheriff and he told me. Why did I have to wait a week to find out about it? I think of myself as part of the family."

What could I say?

"You *are* part of our family, Brent," I said, adding to myself, *So much a part that you usually show up in time for dinner.*

"I wasn't seriously injured, and the car is being repaired as we speak."

He settled himself in the rocker. Misty broke from the pack to leap into his lap where she was always welcome, and my timid Sky lay at his feet as comfortable as if she were one of his own dogs.

"If anything like that happens again, you'll be the first to know," I promised.

"I don't understand," he said. "You're a good driver, and we didn't get much snow."

"What did Crane tell you?"

"That you skidded on the road and went over a cliff."

"That's kind of what happened. First, I had to take a detour, then I found myself on an unfamiliar road and was distracted."

"Some distraction."

"There's more to it than that."

Brent was one of the few people in Foxglove Corners who believed in supernatural manifestations, having experienced them himself. I told him about the sleigh.

"So we're right smack in the middle of a haunting again," he said.

"Well, *I* am. This may be a one-time-only apparition. We're several miles from Windemere Road."

"I'm surprised the sheriff lets you drive at night," he said. "It's dangerous. Will, over at my barn, collided with a deer the other night. The deer didn't make it."

I bristled. Every now and then, Brent, like Lieutenant Mac Dalby, showed his chauvinistic side.

"I wasn't out gallivanting," I said, "and Crane doesn't interfere with my career."

Abruptly, Brent brought the subject back to the apparition.

"I never heard of a ghost sleigh haunt in Foxglove Corners," he said. "Are you going to try to find out if there really was a sleigh with four people in it?"

"There must have been, but who knows if there's a record of it? I didn't find anything about it on the Internet, but I'll go to the library as soon as I have time. Miss Eidt has an extension collection of clippings. She calls the file 'Haunted Corners'."

"It makes you wonder," he said. "What did the four riders do in life that they have to ride through the snow for all eternity?"

He had a good point. Why had I never thought of it?

Six

"It's like the Flying Dutchman," Brent said. "The people on the sleigh want the ride to end, but it never does."

And it never would. Doomed forever to sail the seas. Riding forever on snowy lanes, destined never to go home. The parallels were clear and unsettling.

"That reminds me of a story I read about a group of people who were ordered to stop dancing," I said. "I don't remember why. Maybe to go to church and pray. Anyway, they disobeyed, and as a punishment they were doomed to continue dancing."

"Forever?"

"I think for all their lives. They were known throughout the land by the agitation of their limbs."

"That sounds like one of those scary fairy tales." Brent paused. "And what does that have to do with a sleigh?"

"You asked why the phantom sleigh had to keep moving."

"Oh, yeah. What they did wrong. If they show up again, you can ask them."

Another car door slammed, and once again, the collies flew into motion, this time in a rush to the side door through which Crane always entered the house.

"The sheriff's here," Brent announced. "Now we can eat."

I rose to greet my husband, wading through eight collies to reach him. Like Brent, he brought layers of snow in with him. It blended into the silver streaks that gave his blond hair a distinguished look.

I took his jacket, and snow flew in all directions. "Brent came to visit us," I said.

"I saw the Plymouth."

Brent had the only car in the county with fins.

"Fowler." Crane locked his gun in its cabinet. "I knew I'd find you here."

"I came for dinner," Brent said. "It's...Let's see if I can guess. Pot roast and pie. I'll say apple."

"You'll be wrong. It's pumpkin."

"Good enough."

"I hope so."

While the men talked, I fed the dogs, set the table, and lit the tapers in the heirloom candlesticks that had belonged to Crane's Civil War-era ancestress, Rebecca Ferguson.

One week ago, I had been too close to death for comfort. This evening I was safe in my home, surrounded by my collies, my husband, and our good friend. Fate had served me the American dream on a golden platter and added leaping flames in the fireplace for good measure.

I couldn't be more grateful for my life.

Let me always be this happy, I thought.

~ * ~

Everywhere I went I heard jingle bells. At school, on a girl's reindeer sweater; on the radio, in a rollicking version of *Jingle Bell Rock*; and hanging on the door of a shop where Leonora and I stopped to buy old-time Christmas ornaments on sale. Most of all, at night when I slept.

In my dreams, sleigh bells rang through the snow. Clear, merry, and festive, they began as tinny, imperceptible notes, growing louder as they came closer. There was no way to escape them.

Before I saw the sleigh apparition, I'd planned to make jingle bell collars for the dogs to wear on Christmas day, but the idea had lost its luster.

Another week went by.

My life resumed its familiar pattern on the day I picked up my car which, in my critical eye, was as good as new. Like a novice with her first car, I wanted to go everywhere and do everything at once.

In the end, I decided to visit Annica who worked at Clovers on Saturday morning, then go to the library and begin my research. I took care of the dogs, then headed for Crispian Road, watching for leaping deer and lost sleighs.

The green clovers on the little restaurant's border had a freshly painted glow in the morning light. As I opened the door, clover chimes announced my entrance. Bells were ringing everywhere in the world, it seemed, but these were happy sounds.

Annica, like a ray of sunshine with her red-gold hair and jeweled Christmas tree earrings, looked up from the white-frosted star cookies she was placing in the dessert carousel.

"Hey, Jennet," she said. "I was going to call you. I heard what happened."

"From Brent, I'll bet. Did he tell you everything?"

"Every ghostly thing. But I want to hear it from you."

My favorite booth with the best view of the woods across the road happened to be empty. I sat and admired the candy cane centerpiece with a Santa Claus figure carrying evergreen branches.

"Mary Jeanne is experimenting with Christmas coffeecakes today," Annica said. "Let's try her latest with tea. Marcy will cover for me, and you can fill me in on the haunted sleigh. I gave our new mystery a name," she added.

"I may never see it again."

"Is that what you think?"

Keeping in mind that Foxglove Corners was like a second home to denizens from the world beyond, I said, "Not really."

"Then we have a mystery."

She left me to peruse a menu of the day's desserts and returned with two slices of coffeecake and our tea.

She tapped one earring and the tiny ornaments on the Christmas tree moved. "Okay. Now, what happened? Don't leave anything out."

I told my story again. Her eyes lit up as I described the scene, then grew somber when I included the aftermath.

"You were so lucky," she said. "I'm always afraid of something like that happening. The roads I take have several deep plunges like the one you fell down."

"I guess I can say 'all's well that ends well'."

I broke off a chunk of coffee cake with my fork and tasted it. It was light and sweet, flavored with cinnamon. Mary Jeanne was a master baker.

"Isn't it unusual to see four ghosts in one sighting?" Annica asked.

"And don't forget two horses and a dog. In the past, I've always seen one spirit, one at a time."

"They usually want something, don't they? Like to rest in peace or right a wrong?"

"I'm not an expert, but I'd say there's a good reason for a ghost to walk or, in this case, to ride. You'd think they'd be happy just to wander around in heaven."

"If that's what happens when we die," Annica said. "I don't like to think about it." She tasted her own coffeecake. "Delectable! Okay, you said the four people in the sleigh looked happy. Why not? What's more fun than a sleigh ride? What could their problem be?"

"I can't imagine."

"But you're curious."

"Naturally."

"Then let's find out. I'll help you," she added. "To start, can you connect them to a certain year?"

"That wouldn't be possible, but I had a sense they don't belong to our time. They were all bundled up, so clothing didn't help."

"They're not going to be easy to trace," Annica said.

"Did I mention that one of the men was especially handsome?"

"You left that out."

"You know, you see two men, but for some reason, you're drawn to one."

"Chemistry," she murmured.

"Yes, I wish I'd known him when he was alive."

"For that, you'd have to go back in time."

I couldn't help but smile at the thought. In Foxglove Corners, time travel was possible, but like an apparition, you couldn't count on it happening. You lost your hold on time when you least expected to, when driving on Huron Court. Even then, you couldn't reserve a specific year or even be sure whether you landed in the past or future.

What I *could* do was search through Miss Eidt's 'Haunted Corners' file. A trip to the library was next on my agenda.

Seven

Any one of the elegant Victorian houses on Park Street could have inspired a nostalgic Norman Rockwell winter scene. The Foxglove Corners Public Library was no exception. Once the family home of the town's librarian, Elizabeth Eidt, the library possessed every fancy embellishment a lover of Victoriana could desire.

Multi-colored outdoor lights strung in the front yard's evergreens gave a festive touch to the landscaping, and a fresh balsam wreath adorned with pinecones and red ribbon greeted the visitor as he opened the door.

I breathed in its spicy fragrance and stepped inside out of the cold. In the library, red poinsettia plants were placed at intervals. A live Fraser fir, as yet undecorated, stood in the center of the room. The warm air smelled like Christmas cookies baking in the oven, but most likely it was potpourri.

In the spirit of the season, Miss Eidt's cat, Blackberry, wore a red plaid ribbon around her neck. Never the friendliest of animals, she dashed in front of me and out of sight.

Lucky for her, I wasn't superstitious.

I went first to the dollhouse. A miniature version of the white Victorian-turned-library, it sat on its own table in a bed of artificial snow. I marveled at the tiny furnishings and decorations so lovingly arranged in the small rooms.

The living room had a fireplace with minute candles on the mantel and red stockings hanging below it. A tiny Christmas tree with tinier packages, a sled with a red bow tied around it, a plate of cookies on a side table for Santa--the dollhouse had everything a real house would have including the doll family: mother, father, daughter, son, black cat, and shaggy dog.

As a child, I'd had many toys, including dolls, but never a dollhouse. A sudden sense of loss overwhelmed me. I had to get a grip and tell myself that I didn't really want one.

"Isn't it a charmer?" Debbie, Miss Eidt's young assistant, stood next to me. She reached into the living room and moved a thumb-sized floor lamp to the other side of the loveseat. "I can imagine walking right into it like Alice through the Looking Glass. The kids love it," she added. "Everybody does."

"There's something magical about a dollhouse," I said.

Miss Eidt came out of her office carefully carrying a box. Dressed in cheery holiday red, she greeted me and lifted the top to reveal the dozen treasures within.

"These are old ornaments from Germany," she said. "They're family heirlooms and very, very fragile. Don't you just love this time of year?"

"It's wonderful," I said.

Miss Eidt appeared to have found the fountain of youth. Every time I saw her, she looked younger. These days she wore brighter colors, had a shorter, more youthful hairstyle, and had acquired a collection of jeweled Christmas-themed pins to wear with her pearl necklaces.

I set the box from Clovers on the desk. "This coffeecake is from Mary Jeanne at Clovers. She wouldn't let me pay for it."

"How generous. I'll send her a thank you note."

"The library looks spectacular," I said.

"Wait till we decorate the tree. Now, what can I help you with today?"

"I'd like to go through your vertical files," I said. "I'm on the trail of another ghost. That is, four ghosts."

"Multiple spirits! How exciting!"

"I thought I might find something relevant in the 'Haunted Corners' file."

"I want to hear all about it, but not here," she said. "Let's go to my office."

Responding to a wordless request, Debbie took her place at the main desk.

Inside the office, Miss Eidt plugged in the electric teakettle and cut the string on the box from Clovers. Mary Jeanne had decorated the coffeecake with a whimsical snowman balancing a red cardinal in his branch hand.

"This is too pretty to cut into, but..." She picked up a server decorated with holly berries. "That's why it was made."

"Just a sliver for me," I said as I shrugged out of my parka and settled it over my shoulders. "I already had a slice."

"What kind of ghost did you encounter this time?" Miss Eidt asked.

"Four people riding in a sleigh, two horses, and a Lassie dog," I said.

"You're always seeing dogs."

I nodded. "And they're always collies."

Even in the afterworld, collies knew a friend when they met one.

"Imagine a Christmas card come to life," I said.

Once again, I told the story of the sleigh that had materialized through falling snow on Windemere Road. I omitted my plunge down the incline, however, not wanting to upset Miss Eidt, who took her friends' misfortunes to heart.

"Well," she said when I'd finished, "I've heard of a ghost train but never a ghost sleigh."

"An entire train?"

"So they say. It's been seen on the west side of the Corners. Occasionally, people hear its whistle, but only a few have seen the train itself. The tracks are still there but no longer in use. In fact, they're deteriorating." She brought out two cups and filled the teapot with loose English Breakfast. "Do you suppose your sleigh only comes in the winter?"

"Probably. No one takes a sleigh out in the summertime."

I was going to say that no one takes a sleigh out in any season, but that was wrong. Brent Fowler had an old-fashioned sleigh. He used it to deliver gifts to needy children on Christmas Eve, and Horace Larkin took passengers on a tour of historic houses in a sleigh. There were at least two farms that rented sleighs to customers looking for an unusual winter treat.

But as a general rule, sleighs were as outmoded as Brent's long-finned Plymouth Belvedere.

I glanced at the vertical files off to the side of the office, eager to start my research, but Miss Eidt was in a talkative mood. Taking advantage of it, I asked her about her gentleman friend.

"Have you seen Chester Maywood lately?"

"Oh, yes. Frequently."

"In the library?"

"Yes, and he's escorted me to several events. We've had dinner together. Chester is a marvelous companion."

"It's going well, then?"

"Very well."

She turned her attention to her second piece of coffeecake.

At times, Miss Eidt could be secretive, but her new appearance and demeanor gave voice to everything she wasn't saying.

I drank the rest of my tea, and she rose. "I'll leave you to your research, Jennet. I hope you find your sleigh."

~ * ~

So many ghosts were floating around Foxglove Corners that I was surprised I was the only one seeing them. Along with accounts of traditional sightings, I found a feature story dealing with the phantom train Miss Eidt had mentioned.

She'd omitted the gruesome fact that a man had met his death on the abandoned tracks in the nineteen-forties. Evidence suggested that he had been run over by a train...a train that existed only in the other world. It was the decade's most talked-about mystery.

I suspected something else must have killed him because a ghost train was hardly malevolent. On the other hand, a sleigh had almost been the cause of my death.

'Almost' being the operative word. I had survived.

Still, I preferred to think of spirits as pitiful beings who needed help to achieve peace and happiness in the afterlife. A vengeful ghost was the stuff of nightmares and horror movies.

For an hour, I sifted through Miss Eidt's collection but didn't find even a hint of a phantom sleigh. The time I'd allotted myself for research had slipped away from me. I needed to stop at Blackbourne's Grocers. That done, I'd give the dogs their walks and attention.

I returned the clippings and copies to their respective folders, rinsed my cup, and left the library quietly. I didn't see either Miss Eidt or Debbie, but one of them had begun to decorate the tree.

I still thought I'd find the answers I sought in the library. Only obviously, I hadn't looked in the right place today.

Eight

Have yourself a merry little Christmas...

Once a year the staff of Marston High School came together to celebrate the season of goodwill with a Christmas breakfast in the cafeteria. The first three classes of the day were shortened to allow for a noon dismissal, which meant that many students took the day off.

I had planned accordingly, giving a Christmas slant to my lessons.

Teachers wore gaudy Christmas sweaters or dressy ones with festive touches. Leonora's sweater was green; mine was red. We'd both pinned on sparkly holiday brooches.

Unobtrusive Christmas music played in the background.

Do you see what I see?

The men competed with one another to see who wore the fanciest tie. Everyone would receive a gift from his or her Secret Santa. Afterwards, after the last bell rang to signal dismissal, we could look forward to a long vacation.

Naturally, the mood was merry, and even Principal Grimsley assumed his rarely-seen benevolent persona. If only we could hold onto the spirit throughout the new year.

Leonora and I shed our outwear on a long table at the back of the cafeteria and found seats with women from the History Department. Over pancakes with bacon or scrambled eggs, served by volunteers from the Student Council in elf costumes, we exchanged school gossip and holiday plans.

We seldom had an opportunity just to relax and talk, to socialize. Grimsley gave a speech that was part pep talk and mercifully short, and the elves distributed Secret Santa gifts.

My present from Carol, the new art teacher, took me aback. It was a hand-painted sleigh ornament. From her seat across the room, Carol was looking at me. Hoping my face didn't betray my chagrin, I lifted the sleigh up so she could see it and smiled.

"How pretty," Leonora said. "I have an ornament, too."

Hers was a small diorama with a Nativity scene set against a forest background.

"It's like Carol knew about the phantom sleigh," I said. "But how could she?"

"It's a coincidence. Ornaments are popular gifts."

"But a sleigh?"

"I didn't tell a soul," Leonora said.

"The present I gave was a book of Christmas poetry." I ran my hand over the sleigh's side. Made of china, it was heavy, perhaps too heavy for a slender balsam branch. "If I were superstitious, I'd think this was a sign."

"A sign of what?"

I frowned. I had told myself I wasn't superstitious at the library the other day when Blackberry crossed my path.

Okay. Maybe I *was*.

"A sign that the apparition isn't through with me."

"That," Leonora said, "is nonsense. It may be, it may not be, but it's not up to a decoration."

"I think I should make another trip to Windemere Road," I said.

~ * ~

Windemere Road lay still and silent under a dusting of snow. I drove past the curves and brought the car to a stop on the verge. At this point, the land had risen until it was almost level with the adjacent ground.

Nothing stirred except waves of wind-driven snow blowing under a cold gray sky. What had compelled me to revisit this isolated area today?

"I see plenty of tracks out there," Leonora pointed out. "None of them were made by a sleigh."

"They're animal tracks. Deer from the woods and some other creature. Coyotes probably."

"The sleigh is somewhere else today," she added.

"I wonder if I'll ever see it again."

My eyes focused on the road ahead and the distant golden blur slowly taking shape. Barking shattered the stillness.

It came closer, resolving itself into a running dog.

As it drew nearer, I noted its sable coat, white ruff, and blaze. It was a collie. Another moment, and it would reach us, sit and lift its paw in true Lassie fashion.

"It's the dog who ran with the sleigh," I said.

"He doesn't look like a ghost to me. I hope he's friendly."

The dog kept running as if afraid the car would disappear. Was he in trouble? Was that why I'd felt compelled to return to Windemere Road today?

I rejected the idea out of hand. Rescue didn't work that way.

Having reached its destination, the dog jumped up on the side of the car, inches from my face. His tail was wagging, but he was panting heavily, and his dark eyes were alive with pleading. I wondered how long he'd been running.

"Uh oh," Leonora said. "Rescuer on the job."

My Lassie dog was filthy, his fur dull and covered with burrs that always manage to survive snow and cold. Under a bedraggled coat, his ribs were plainly visible.

I had the tools of the trade in my trunk: canine first aid kit, collar and leash, blankets, bottled water, bowls, and an assortment of canine treats—everything I could possibly need to lure a reluctant dog to safety.

I wouldn't need them for the collie.

When I opened the door, Lassie jumped into my lap. A good seventy pounds of collie with muddy paws settled happily onto my purple parka and a good portion of my dress beneath. In a collie's effortless attempt to be adorable, he licked my hand.

His collar was a thin rope. Attached to it was an index card with a few blurred words in ink on it: *My name is Nova.*

"Nova," I murmured. "Someone gave you a lovely name but didn't keep you."

"How sad for him," Leonora said. "So close to Christmas, too."

"Dogs don't know holidays," I said. "And this is a her."

I had to get her off my lap. I shoved her gently aside, then went back to the trunk. She followed me, observing as I selected a bottle of water, a bowl, and a package of treats from my supply. Liver—ugh.

She licked her chops.

When the package was empty and she'd had her fill of water, I spread a blanket on the back seat. Nova lost no time in lying on her makeshift bed.

"She must have been drinking snow, but she can't have found much to eat except wildlife," I said. "It depends how long she was on her own."

"Are we taking her to Sue Appleton?" Leonora asked.

"No, to Brent's barn. He volunteered to foster collies for the League."

Nova was already asleep. There is no trust like that of a dog.

"She's going to love Brent," I said.

~ * ~

On the way to Brent's barn, I kept remembering my first sight of the dog who ran with the sleigh. The Lassie dog. I'd assumed she was part of the apparition. But I'd seen it for the merest fragment of a moment.

Obviously, the dog who slept in the back seat of my car wasn't a phantom. But could she have been aware of the sleigh? I imagined her on her own in the snowy wilderness, hungry for food and attention, hearing the sleigh bells and seeing four humans in a moving vehicle, along with another dog who looked like her.

My white collie, Misty, had often set one foot in the other world. I called her my psychic collie. Perhaps Nova was similarly talented.

And what of the people, the riders I had come to think of as the Christmas revelers? Could they be modern day party-goers, donned in period costume for an old-fashioned sleigh ride?

Almost certainly not. Still...I wanted to think more about this but now wasn't the time. I needed to be alone in quiet surroundings where I could replay the experience and ponder its significance. And Brent's barn was just ahead.

"Brent's there," Leonora said. "Good."

His vintage Plymouth was parked alongside a flatbed truck. Sensing that we'd reached our destination, Nova woke and stared out the window. She started whining as Brent came out to greet us, backed up by his collie pack.

I opened the door and led her outside. Brent's dogs barked, whether welcome or warning I couldn't tell. Outnumbered, Nova instantly pressed against me.

"Who's this?" Brent asked.

"I brought you a dog to foster. Her name is Nova."

He held out his palm for Nova to sniff. The barking grew louder. I imagined Brent's dogs were reluctant to share their master's attention.

"She was running loose on Windemere Road with only this pathetic rope for a collar," I said.

"Windemere? Is that on your way home?"

"School's out for Christmas vacation," Leonora said. "We thought we'd celebrate by taking a little ride."

Brent saw through her excuse. He turned to me. "This looks like the dog you saw running with the sleigh."

"It looks like her, yes."

"Then that sleigh...Was it a real one after all?"

"No, only the dog is real," I said.

"I don't understand what's going on out here, but let's not stand around in the cold." He beckoned to Nova. "Welcome, Nova. How would you like a little dinner?"

Ah, the words every dog wants to hear.

She followed him into the barn. So did we.

Nine

Brent lived in a grand house on Wolf Lake Road, but his barn was his second home. Here his horses were stabled and his dogs had a fenced-in meadow for running or playing or napping in the sun.

Two large Christmas wreaths decorated with red ribbons and bells hung on the door. It was a warm and welcoming place.

Will, the young man who'd had the run-in with the deer, set a pail he was carrying on the wood floor. Husky and light-haired with a wholesome country appearance, he had the open smile of a youth who has never met adversity.

"Lassie," he said on seeing Nova.

Everyone who keeps a collie must have heard that name come his way at some time or other.

"Meet our new arrival, Nova," Brent said. To Leonora and me, he added, "This may be my first foster, but I know what to do."

"Exactly what is that?" Leonora asked, with a teasing glint in her eyes.

"Provide water first and kibble. I have Doctor Alice on speed dial. After Nova is settled in, I just let her be a collie until somebody shows up to adopt her."

"You're forgetting," I said. "You have to keep Nova away from your dogs until Alice gives you the all clear."

"Got it covered." Brent led Nova to a crate set up in a quiet, private corner of the barn. "In you go, girl."

Will set a bowl of water inside the crate. At a makeshift counter, he poured kibble into a bowl. "One cup, boss?"

"For now," Brent said. "Tell me, Jennet. You found this collie where the ghost sleigh ran you off the road. How do you explain that?"

"It's a coincidence," I said. "The apparition and the abandoned dog are separate..." I searched in vain for the right word. "Entities? Issues? Problems?"

Will reached in the crate to stroke Nova's head before serving her dinner. She leaned against the door. She was as hungry for attention as for food.

She ate daintily, lying down with one paw resting on the edge of the dish as if to keep it from vanishing. The kibble was soon gone.

Jeff, another one of Brent's men, came up to greet the new arrival. "That doesn't seem like enough food for a starving dog."

In my opinion, it was just enough, keeping in mind the treats she'd devoured. "She can have more later."

We watched as, apparently satisfied, Nova curled up into a fluffy ball and closed her eyes.

"She'll need a bath," Jeff said. "I'll take of that."

"Do you girls have time for coffee?" Brent asked.

I spied the half-filled box of doughnuts next to the coffeemaker. How long had it been since our festive breakfast?

"That sounds good," I said.

Brent poured coffee into three mugs. "I'm still not clear, Jennet. Was there a dog in your apparition or not?"

"I don't know. All I can say is that I saw one dog running in front of the sleigh, and she looked like Nova."

"The mystery deepens," Leonora said.

"All right." Brent took a long gulp of his coffee which was amazing as it was so hot. "When you figure it out, let me know."

"I will. In the meantime, I'll contact Sue. After Alice vets Nova, Sue will take her picture and do a short write up for the website."

"I'd like to keep Nova here for Christmas," he said. "We're going to have a party at the barn for the men and the animals. You ladies are both invited."

"Wow!" Leonora said. "Will we fit in, do you think?"

I thanked him for both of us. "It'll be fun. Now, we'd better be on our way."

I would have given Nova a farewell pat but didn't want to disturb her as she had fallen asleep. Still, I said, "Goodbye for now, Nova. You're in a good place."

And we'd done a good day's rescue work.

~ * ~

Christmas is coming, the goose is getting fat...

'Twas the season to hear Christmas music in every store and restaurant in Foxglove Corners. And bells. It seemed that bells followed me around, evoking visions of the phantom sleigh.

Well, it was also the season of bells.

Now that I didn't have to go to school, I could resume my search for a documented apparition similar to the one I'd seen.

Annica and I sat in a coffee bar at the Maplegrove Mall taking a break from Christmas shopping. I had a long list and so far, only two presents bought: an antique music box for Aunt Becky, and a frilly white blouse for my sister, Julia.

Annica was looking for a gift for Brent. Naturally, it had to be perfect.

"He has everything," she said. "Or he could buy it."

She was wearing the emerald earrings Brent had given her last Christmas with a green turtleneck sweater. I knew what she was thinking. How could a college student who worked as a waitress top that?

The answer was simple. She couldn't. She shouldn't even try. Annica was missing the point of Christmas gift giving.

"That's true, but he'll love whatever you give him because it's from you," I said.

"But what can I buy him? It has to be special and romantic."

"That's a tall order. Could you make something for him?"

"I'm not clever. It has to be super special."

"We'll keep looking. There's a store here, Wood Works. Maybe you can find a figure of a horse—or a fox."

"That isn't romantic. Brent invited me to the New Year's Eve party at the Hunt Club Inn," she added.

"That'll be fun. Leonora and I got an invitation to the barn."

Annica was staring over my shoulder. "Isn't that Lucy Hazen out in the mall?"

It was indeed. Foxglove Corners' celebrated writer sat at a bench in front of Santa's Castle. I was used to seeing Lucy dressed in black, in her own background, the atmospheric house known as Dark Gables. She was wearing a long black coat with a red scarf. No doubt she had a matching dress under it and a number of gold chains.

Annica sprang up. "I'll ask her to join us."

I watched as Lucy rose and accompanied Annica back to the coffee bar. An idea that had been lurking in the back of my mind pushed itself forward.

Along with being an accomplished and popular writer, Lucy had other talents. At times, her second sense came into play, giving her a glimpse of future events. She read tea leaves, had premonitions, and generously shared her vast knowledge of the supernatural.

Why hadn't I told her about the apparition? Now was my chance.

"Are you Christmas shopping, Lucy?" I asked as she joined us at the table.

"I'm observing people, shopping for ideas," she said. "Did you ever think there could be anything sinister about Santa's Castle?"

"Not really," Leonora said.

"Except it can be scary for a little kid. Look at that child crying. She's afraid of Santa Claus. I ask myself, why?"

"And you have a story," I said.

"An idea." She glanced at my plate. "Is that a cinnamon roll?"

"Yes, it's delicious."

"I think I'll have one. Tell me, what's new with you girls?"

"We have a new mystery," Annica said. "That is, Jennet does. I'm going to help her solve it."

"Is it a Christmas mystery?" Lucy asked.

"In a way." I told her about the sleigh apparition, including my narrow escape.

"That's extremely odd," she said. "You saw four people?"

"And their two horses."

I had to tell Nova's story then from our first sight of her, running toward us on Windemere Road, to our last glimpse of her safe in Brent's care.

"What do you make of it?" I asked.

"I'm not sure. You could have been killed, but that doesn't mean the ghosts meant to harm you."

"What did they think was going to happen?"

Did spirits retain their ability to reason? To formulate a plan and put it into motion? I didn't think so, but I wasn't an expert.

"It's complicated," she said. "Let me think about it. In the meantime, stay away from Windemere Road."

Ten

The library sat quietly in a bed of fresh snow with only the walkway shoveled. It was ten o'clock, opening time, and an unusual hour for me to embark on a search through Foxglove Corners' past. But Christmas was coming and the goose was getting fat. I had to use every available moment before holiday madness took over my life.

The box of doughnuts from the Hometown Bakery should cheer Miss Eidt and give me the energy to stay with my task until I found the phantom sleigh.

Once again, Blackberry dashed in front of me and vanished in a blur of black fur and red ribbon. Miss Eidt had strung fairy lights around the dollhouse, and the Fraser fir sparkled with old-time ornaments and tinsel.

Most Christmas trees in public places were decorated with inexpensive colored balls. I hoped Miss Eidt was keeping an eye on her priceless heirlooms lest some wayward child break one.

"Merry Christmas, Jennet," Miss Eidt said, her gaze on the bakery box. "I see you bought a gift."

"The best," I said. "Doughnuts."

"They're most happily received."

Her dress was royal blue, and she wore a jeweled bauble on a silver chain in place of her signature pearls.

"Aren't you busy getting ready for the holiday?" she asked.

Visions of Christmas gifts unpurchased and cookies unbaked danced through my head. "I'm multi-tasking," I said. "I'd like to search the vertical files again. I might have missed something. First, I'll see if there's anything new in the Gothic Nook."

"You're in luck. Debbie and I went to a half-price bookstore in Maple Creek yesterday. We found a ton of Gothics, all in good condition. They're still on the cart."

"Great. I'll check them out."

"And I'll put the kettle on." She took possession of the bakery box.

Even the Gothic Nook had its special touch of Christmas with a collection of Santas from around the world scattered on tables and shelves. A Father Christmas figure dressed in blues, white, and silver caught my attention, first because of his glitter-sprinkled robes, then because of his expression. It was the polar opposite of benevolent.

I stared at it, remembering Lucy's comment about a crying child at the Santa Castle. The figure's expression appeared to change the longer you looked at it, to become almost threatening. In what country would he be popular?

"Season's greetings, Jennet!"

Edwina Endicott entered the Nook silently, looking like a wraith in winter white wool with a silver snowflake brooch pinned to the bodice of her dress.

"Same to you," I said.

"Look what I found in the new fiction." She held up a book with a cheery fireplace scene on the cover. Its title was anything but cheery: *Ten Horror Stories for Christmas.*

"That's not my cup of tea," I murmured.

"Oh, but Christmas is the perfect time for spirits to roam."

Edwina must not be familiar with Shakespeare's thoughts on the subject: *No fairy takes, nor witch hath power to charm...*

"Imagine the Ghost of Christmas Future leading you to a grave and seeing your own name on the headstone," she said. "How cool would that be?"

"It'd be ghastly. Fortunately, *A Christmas Carol* doesn't end there."

"The ghosts are active in real life, too," she said. "I live near Huron Court, and I like to take early morning walks in the snow. You'll never guess who I saw the other day."

I was certain I knew. "Violet Randall with her dog."

"You're good, Jennet. That's who I think they were. She was carrying a basket. I called out to her, but she kept walking. Then the wind blew snow over the road, and I lost her."

"Weather is a spirit's best friend," I said. "Mist or fog or blowing snow lets them disappear at will."

"Are you doing anything exciting for Christmas?" she asked.

"We're having company from out of town. How about you?"

"It'll be quiet." Her gaze fell on the cart of Gothics waiting to be shelved. I'd better take what I wanted quickly before she scooped them all up.

But my inner voice was trying desperately to be heard. *Ask her*, it insisted. *What do you have to lose?*

I said, "Speaking of Christmas ghosts, did you ever hear or read about a phantom sleigh with four people in it?"

"Are you thinking of the phantom train?"

"No, this was a horse-drawn sleigh. And a collie running with it."

I went into more detail than I'd originally intended. It was as if an alien spirit had taken control of my tongue.

I found myself talking about the Christmas colors of the girls' scarves and coats, of the evergreen roping on the sides of the sleigh, and the bells but stopped myself when I began to describe the handsome man.

I told her everything except for the fact that I was the one who had seen the sleigh and that it had forced me off the road.

"That's a fascinating story. Where did you hear about it?"

"From someone. I don't remember exactly."

"It rings a bell." She giggled at her word choice. "Oh, not literally. I can't tell you about your joyriding spirits, but I remember an account I came across about a very strange disappearance. A sleigh, together with its four passengers and horses, went missing one Christmas Eve. This happened many years ago. They were never found."

That's it! My apparition.

"We heard the same story. How many years ago did this happen?"

"Decades. The nineteen twenties or thirties."

"And four people disappeared...at once?"

"As I recall there were two couples. They were never seen again. Neither was their sleigh or their animals."

Well, then...

I had been looking in the wrong place. I should search for disappearances in Foxglove Corners.

"Do you remember their names?"

"Sorry. I can't help you. But I'm pretty sure they vanished from Foxglove Corners. May I ask why you're interested?"

"You may."

I didn't want to discuss my ghostly sighting with anyone except my closest friends. Edwina had a tendency to gossip and often made snide remarks about how I had taken Foxglove Corners' most eligible bachelor out of circulation.

"Christmas and sleighs go together," I said. "I received a sleigh ornament as an early present. I'm thinking about starting a collection."

That statement had more than a grain of truth in it.

"Sleighs are cool," she said. "It's so much more elegant to skim across a snowy road than to tear up the land in an ATV. Well, let's see what they have here."

We both turned to the cart and made our selections. The three paperbacks I chose looked good, but I could hardly wait to sift through Miss Eidt's collection of news stories. I had a feeling that Edwina had pointed me in the right direction.

"Have a lovely Christmas, Edwina," I said with more warmth than I usually sent her way and left her still looking through the books on the cart.

Eleven

Over the years an incredible number of people had gone missing in Foxglove Corners. The number seemed particularly overwhelming to me since I was writing their names in my notebook.

I knew the story of Brandymere. According to legend, unwary travelers, whether on foot or behind the wheel of a car, invariably reached a point where they dropped off the face of the earth and were seen no more.

Crane claimed it was all nonsense. He had driven up and down Brandymere for years and never disappeared. Needless to say, I hadn't been tempted to see if I could do the same and survive the experience.

Huron Court was another road best avoided, as I and my friends had learned to our dismay. Here the season could change in the blink of an eye, sweet-scented summer air filling with winter snow without warning. Another road to avoid. Along with Windemere, the route favored by the phantom sleigh, although perhaps I was the only one who knew of its danger.

The stories of the vanished ones were eerily similar. One young woman left a party alone and never returned home. Another, a child, was seen boarding a school bus, but when all the children had been dropped off at their stops, she wasn't to be found. Had she disappeared from inside the bus? How could that happen? Whatever her fate, her grieving parents never found her.

A young wife failed to return home from a trip to the grocery store. All indications were that she planned to come back, put the clean laundry in the dryer, and run the vacuum which had been left plugged in, in the middle of the living room.

I added her name, Faith Landry, to my growing list and set my notebook to one side.

"Would you like more tea, Jennet?" Miss Eidt opened the door, her eyes taking in the papers I'd spread across the table. "We can finish the doughnuts."

"I'm ready for a break," I said. "I've learned that we live in a dangerous town, Miss Eidt. People are constantly disappearing."

"Surely you exaggerate."

"I have seven names on one page, all of people who vanished from this area in the past two years. How do you explain that?"

"Alien abduction?"

"Seriously."

She filled the teakettle. "This can happen in any town, not just in Foxglove Corners. It could also be that some people want to disappear."

She glanced at the names written on my page. "Faith Landry, for example. I'm familiar with her story. She was a newlywed. Who's to say that she didn't realize she made a mistake and just quietly left her old life to start a new one?"

"But what about the little girl who went missing from inside a bus?"

"I won't touch that one." She looked again at my notebook. "Did you find what you were looking for?"

"No, and it shouldn't be so hard. How often do four people disappear at the same time?"

"From a tour, maybe."

"From a sleigh ride in Foxglove Corners."

I glanced at my watch. I could stay in the library for another hour; then I had to go home. I felt that I would be taking the burden of all these unsolved cold cases with me. If only I could solve one. My own case.

"Have another doughnut," Miss Eidt said. "Let your cares drift away. Think about Christmas and candlelight and stars…"

She passed the bakery box to me, and I made my choice. While eating it, I added my own list of wonderful things: Bells…Church bells. Jingle bells. Sleigh bells. A bell decoration on an orange-glazed doughnut.

Surely I'd find an account of the missing foursome if I kept looking. Edwina couldn't have made the story up out of whole cloth.

~ * ~

Success! An hour later I found two yellowing articles clipped together in the last folder I opened. One had likely been taped to a sheet of heavy off-white paper, suggesting it had originally come from a scrapbook.

The facts were as Edwina remembered them. Four young people had embarked on a Christmas Eve sleigh ride from which they never returned. Nor was the sleigh ever found; nor did the horses return to their stables.

The date of the fatal ride was December 24th, 1937. The names of the riders were: Miss Auralee Faraday and Miss Margaret Faraday, cousins; Mr. Nicholas Dover, medical student, and Mr. Edmund Sherman.

The sleigh had set out from Faraday Hill at four-thirty in the afternoon. The feature story, yellowing and tattered at the edges, contained a crude map of Foxglove Corners as it existed in the 1930s.

Foul play was suspected, but nothing was ever proved.

I returned to the articles to make sure I had copied all relevant material into my notebook. The feature story had been written in 1942, five years after the disappearance. At that time, the country was embroiled in World War II. Other news stole the spotlight from a five-year-old cold case.

In all this time, no one had found a trace of the vanished sleigh or its occupants.

I closed the notebook and finished my tea. It had grown cold, and the leftover doughnuts lying a bed of crumbs and sprinkles had lost their appeal.

Where on God's earth could the four sleigh riders have gone? A sleigh needs to move on snow. It couldn't sail to another location or travel out of the state on the roads of the thirties.

Had it ever left Foxglove Corners? Had it skimmed over the snowy roads and found its way to the Twilight Zone? Somehow.

And the riders. In the thirties, at the time of the fateful ride, they were young. How old would they be now? I'd seen them as they had looked on that long-ago Christmas Eve. In another century.

I had no ready answer, but now I knew the names of the young people involved, a place name, Faraday Hill, and I had resources.

I had everything except time.

Christmas is coming...

~ * ~

Miss Eidt said, "I never saw those articles. If I had, I'd have remembered when you told me about the sleigh."

'Local Unsolved Disappearances' was written on the folder in Miss Eidt's hand. Inside were a jumble of loose clippings. Usually, the material she handled was filed in an orderly fashion.

"Who else has access to the vertical file?" I asked.

"Only Debbie. I realize this file is a relic from the past. People today have quicker ways of finding out information. But I intend to keep adding to it for old times' sake, and because it's a hobby of mine. I'll talk to Debbie," she added.

"Would you mind if I make copies of these stories?"

"Of course not, Jennet. Go ahead. I hope they'll help you."

"They may. Also, do you have a map of old Foxglove Corners?"

"That I can give you."

"I want to look up a place called Faraday Hill."

"I've never heard of it."

"With a map, I may be able to find it."

"And then what?"

"We'll see," I said. "I have more than I had before. Now I'll see where it takes me."

Twelve

Annica agreed to help me search for Faraday Hill on the following day as soon as her shift at Clovers was over. I realized that over the years the house—if indeed the name referred to a house—might have been demolished to make way for a newer structure.

If we found it, how would we be able to identify it? But with two maps we should be able to find the general area.

Look for hills, I told myself. *Elementary*.

I didn't expect to find a clue or make a major discovery. I simply hoped to see the part of the county where it had all begun.

I hadn't found obituaries for the four young people, which didn't surprise me as their bodies had never been found. I imagined their families clung to the belief that they'd come home some day with a wild story to explain their disappearance.

And what a story that would be!

But, realistically, how long could one keep hope alive?

Well, that was tomorrow; I needed to make the most of today. I gave the dogs extra attention and playtime, cleaned the guestroom, and decorated the tree. Crane had already strung the lights and set the treetop on the highest branch.

The rich scent of balsam enveloped me as I adorned the branches with stars, bells, snowflakes, angels, small dioramas, and frosted fruits—all the ornaments in our collection.

When the boxes were empty, I reached for the sleigh from my Secret Santa. It was heavier than it had seemed when I'd first unwrapped it. Maybe I'd better find another place for it, like on the mantel. But no... It seemed to demand that I find it a home on the tree.

I did, finally, on a thick lower branch, under a white light where no one could miss it.

There. Done. In time to make dinner.

I glanced out the window. A few snowflakes were drifting down, just enough for holiday atmosphere. I felt happy and satisfied with my day's work.

~ * ~

The next day, Annica and I set out to find a place that might no longer exist. Snow had begun to fall, light flakes that melted when they reached the ground.

This wasn't the best day to look for a road sign, but neither Annica nor I had the luxury of waiting for ideal weather conditions. After today, Annica was working double shifts at Clovers until Christmas Eve, and I still wasn't ready for the holiday.

For some reason, the anniversary of the sleigh's disappearance had acquired the significance of a deadline in my mind. December 24th. Did I have to solve the mystery by then? Or... My mind refused to offer up an alternative.

Deadlines were for projects, like wrapping Christmas gifts, not for uncovering old secrets.

"I found Brent's present," Annica announced, "and it's perfect."

"What is it?" I asked.

"A beer stein with a magnificent castle and the words: *I lost my heart in Heidelberg*. The decoration includes little blue hearts. What do you think?"

"Does Brent drink beer?"

"Not often, but he can use it on his desk or bookcase as a decoration."

"Like I told you, he'll love it because you gave it to him."

"I hope so."

She unfolded the map Miss Eidt had given me. "We're looking for a road called Faraday Hill?"

"I'm not sure it's a road. Maybe it's the name of an estate."

"Roads don't change their names over time, do they?"

"Rarely. To honor an historical figure sometimes. But I wouldn't think that happens in Foxglove Corners."

"There's Spruce Lake Road," she said, "and Spruce Lake Farms. It's so pretty out here. I'd love to come back at night when we could really appreciate the lights and decorations."

"Yes, well, it wouldn't be easy to find what we're looking for in the dark."

Gradually the road sloped upward and the land with it until we were deep in hill country.

What were we looking for? I had created a picture of it in my mind.

It would be a Victorian on a hilltop, aging but still splendid. Like that old white house ahead. I slowed slightly in order to see it more clearly.

It sat proudly on its hill, looking down at the evergreens that marched up to its spacious entrance. It had no holiday decorations but didn't need extraneous ornamentation. The classic lines and extravagance of gingerbread trim were sufficient to make it stand out.

"I'd love to live in a house like that someday," Annica said. "It would be like living on a cloud. You could see everything for miles around."

I smiled at her fancy, thinking about drawbacks such as trudging or driving uphill to the house in winter, in snow or ice. Ice? No one could skate uphill.

"Marry a rich man then," I said.

She held the map closer to her face. "We're close to Fairhill Road. That sounds like Faraday Hill. Almost."

We both looked but either roads weren't named in this area or their signposts were obscured by snowdrifts. We passed more woods, a new development named Frost Lake Estates, and finally came to the lake, a frozen expanse of ice held fast in the embrace of the glistening white woodland behind it.

All it needed were skaters to create a glorious Christmas card scene.

"According to the map from the *Banner*, we're in the right place, but this is a veritable wilderness," I said. "And, darn, it's snowing harder. We'd better turn around while the turning's good."

"I guess, but what a disappointing end to our adventure. I wish we'd found the road the sleigh took."

"Maybe this was it," I said. "So many years ago, they may have been on this very road heading in our direction. They'd have to be to end up on Windemere Road. Now we're going in theirs."

"That was so long ago, before we were born. If this were summer, I think we would have been able to find Faraday Hill."

"It'll be too late then."

Did I say that? Obviously. But why? Where had it come from?

"What do you mean?" Annica asked.

I had to give her an answer. "Just that this is a Christmas mystery."

It was as vague as it could be, but at the same time as good an explanation as any.

Thirteen

The collies loved to play in the snow, especially when it was falling from the sky. Even timid Sky, who was most comfortable lying under the dining room table, dashed around with her sisters, tunneling through snowdrifts with her long nose.

After a morning in the kitchen baking Christmas cookies, I craved fresh air and exercise, even though the dogs were doing the running.

They didn't seem to realize that balls made of snow will melt. They were certain that, sooner or later, they'd catch one and bring it back to me. I love the optimism of the typical dog.

I pitched a snowball farther than I intended to, and the pack raced to the edge of Jonquil Lane. But no farther. Crane had trained them to stop at all roads until given the go-ahead. Velvet, our newest, was the exception. She considered the lane part of her new territory.

Having heard the hum of a motor down the lane, I raced forward myself and grabbed her collar.

"No!" I said firmly. "No road!"

She looked at me and wagged her tail happily. I was going to have to keep her on her leash until we reached an understanding.

Moments later, a vintage white Plymouth Belvedere emerged from the gently falling snow, its long green fins a welcome splash of color in the unrelenting white.

Brent parked behind my car and led Nova out. Immediately, my dogs turned their attention to the new canine in their midst. Brent held onto Nova who eyed them smugly as if to say: *I have a home, too. I belong.*

I gave her a pat, let my hand linger on the top of her blaze. Her fur was so soft and warm—and real. How could I have thought even for a moment that she was part of an apparition?

"She looks great," I said.

"She should after two baths and two massive grooming sessions."

"You'd never know she's been running free."

"I kept that paper tag from her collar," he said. "But I'm sure no one will come looking for her."

"I'm equally sure some heartless fiend turned her loose to fend for herself. Her last home could have been anywhere."

"I took Nova over to see Sue," he said. "I'm keeping her over Christmas. Sue said she's not letting anyone take a dog home until after the new year anyway."

That was Rescue League policy, and a good one. Too many people want a puppy or adult dog for the holidays. Then their interest fades, and the pet ends up discarded like Anderson's little fir tree.

"Nova is a good dog," Brent said. "She's smart, too. She understands everything I tell her."

I had a suspicion that he planned to keep her after the holiday. The two of them looked as if they belonged together, as if they had been man and dog for years.

"They all love her at the barn," he added. "Speaking of which, I came to remind you about the Christmas party. It's tomorrow afternoon, starting at two."

"I'll be there. I can't speak for Leonora."

"It's sort of an open house. There'll be gifts for everyone. Dogs, too."

"Let's go in," I said. "I found out something interesting."

I opened the door, and we all trooped into the mudroom bringing a prodigious amount of snow in with us—more as eight collies shook their coats vigorously. Nova hadn't been outside long enough to acquire more than a light dusting.

The kitchen retained the delicious smell of cookies, and there they were, arranged on their tins waiting to be decorated.

As Velvet placed her front paws on the table, I said, "No!"

That was my cue to spread biscuits from the Lassie tin on a paper for my always-hungry crew, including, of course, Nova, who had been accepted by the pack.

"I came at the right time," Brent said, shrugging out of his jacket. "What kind are they?"

"Just basic Christmas cookies." I took off my parka but kept my boots on as Brent did. "You should visit Camille. She's turning out every variety known to man."

"Maybe I will," he said. "Are they ready to eat?"

"If you don't need colored sugar or frosting. They're still warm."

I set a half dozen unfrosted stars and bells on a plate and filled the coffeemaker. "I'm one step closer to solving the mystery of the sleigh."

I told him what I'd learned in the two articles, and our unsuccessful attempt to find Faraday Hill.

"At least I know who the people were." I repeated their names. "My ghost riders."

"Let me try," he said. "I'll ask Alethea Venn. She lives in Frost Lake Estates."

"Alethea," I murmured, breaking my cookie in half.

Alethea was my second least favorite person in Foxglove Corners, with Veronica the Viper, she who had cast her covetous eye on my husband, topping the list.

Alethea was a wealthy, gorgeous, snippy, red-haired foxhunter who regarded Brent as her personal property. She had no use for those like me whose allegiance lay with the fox.

But if she could help us...Brent would be the one dealing with her.

"Don't tell her about my apparition, whatever you do," I said.

"I'll just say I heard the story and was curious."

"That'll do. It isn't commonly known. I had to plow through a ton of paper to find two little articles. After Christmas, I'll try again."

"Maybe by then, I'll have a location for you, if Alethea comes through," he said.

~ * ~

After dinner, Crane pushed two packages to the back of the tree behind the manger. I didn't see any tags on them so decided they were for me.

Christmas is coming, the goose is getting fat...

"I'm glad I ordered a fresh turkey from Blackbourne's Grocers," I said, the merry Christmas tune running through my head. "I couldn't keep fattening up a goose, knowing I was going to cook it."

My mind slid over the fact that the goose would have to be killed first. By somebody.

Think about cranberries, sweet potatoes and gingerbread instead.

"You're not exactly a pioneer girl," Crane said.

"Not at all. Camille is having the whole family for dinner on Christmas Eve. I'm taking Christmas day."

I'd have a ham with potato salad, biscuits, and all the trimmings which varied from year to year. I was baking cookies for everybody, and Camille was constructing her special Yule logs.

All I had to do was finish my Christmas shopping, wrap presents, and add a few finishing touches to the house's decor...

Stop! commanded my inner voice. *Hang one more swag or ornament, and you'll cross over into Excess Land.*

And take another trip to the mall...That was necessary. I needed to find the perfect gift for Crane.

Tomorrow after he left, I'd have a closer look at the mysterious presents he'd laid under the tree. Maybe I'd shake them. The smaller one could contain jewelry. Crane had excellent taste. The best. I touched the crystal snowflake he had given me.

Misty nudged me with her nose. *Don't forget us.*

I won't," I said, adding a stop at Pluto's Gourmet Pet Shop to next day's list.

Christmas was coming, and I was determined to be ready for it.

~ * ~

Christmas, having monopolized all my daytime thoughts and energy, invaded my dreams.

That night I woke feeling fearful, while the fragments of a particularly vivid dream crashed around me. I was decorating our tree which had, unaccountably, lost its ornaments. I reached for the sleigh from my Secret Santa, surprised that it was as warm as if it had been lying next to the fireplace. As I placed it on a low branch under a white light, it began to glow—and grow.

Come join us, it said.

And that was all.

Fourteen

Come join us.

The words stayed with me the next morning. They amounted to a command, and they'd been voiced by an inanimate object, a Christmas ornament hanging on my own tree.

So, for heaven's sake, don't take them seriously.

It was only a dream, a weird one to be sure, but it held no significance for my future. It was a natural result of being too busy, too preoccupied with Christmas preparations. I'd been thinking about sleighs too much and sampling too many of my cookies.

So I told myself, but the dark invitation haunted me.

Join us...In what place? I could think of only one, and I loved my life in this world too much to leave it willingly.

Brent's party was this afternoon. I'd be going alone as Leonora thought she was coming down with the flu, which meant I had plenty of time to visit Lucy at Dark Gables.

I had to be honest with myself. The dream bothered me. Or maybe it was the mystery of the disappearing sleigh itself. In any event, I needed the assurance of Lucy's input.

~ * ~

Wherever you turned in Foxglove Corners you came across a scene worthy of a Christmas card or the picture on a tin of holiday candy. Lucy's secluded house, Dark Gables, was a prime example. You couldn't see it from the Spruce Road. To visit Lucy, you had to drive down a private road bordered with tall evergreens that held fast to their color in all seasons.

Green and white with splashes of red greeted the visitor, and at the end of the driveway stood Lucy's classic house with the gables that had inspired its name. Lucy had wound roping and ribbon around her lamp post and hung wreaths in every window at the front of the house. Only at this time of year did Dark Gables look cheerful.

Lucy opened the door before I could knock. Her blue merle collie, who shared a name with my Sky, backed up to let me enter, so much more polite than my lunging crew.

"Jennet!" Lucy said. "Come on in out of the cold."

Strangely she wore red instead of black.

As she pulled the door shut and reached for the package of cookies in my hand, the gold charms on her bracelet clanged together. More Christmas cheer.

"How lovely," she said. "We'll have them with our tea."

"I wanted to talk to you about the sleigh," I said. "I have new information. Miss Eidt has a treasure trove in her vertical file, but most people go straight to the Internet."

"This apparition worries you," Lucy said. "It's understandable."

When we were settled in the sunroom with cups of tea and my cookies, I told Lucy what I had learned and ended by mentioning my dream.

She didn't bother to hide her smile. "Your ornament talked to you. That doesn't happen often. 'Come join us.' What do you make of those three words?"

With Lucy I could give voice to my deepest fear. "That they want me to share their fate."

"Which is…"

"Death, obviously."

Lucy took a sip of her tea. "I don't think so. When you told me you dreamed about the sleigh, I assumed you were referring to the apparition. But your dream was about a decoration. It could mean something harmless like *Come join us on the tree.*"

I laughed at the impossibility of that notion.

"Not death then," I said.

"Well, not death by sleigh. If anything, the riders might be hoping you'll find a way to allow them to rest in peace."

"That's a tall order."

"You've done it before."

"This time the mystery is so remote, though. There's hardly any documentation about the phenomenon, let alone the actual event. If there were any clues, someone would have discovered what happened by now."

"It depends how hard they looked at the time," Lucy said. "And for how long."

"I may go back to the library, but after Christmas. Crane's family will be here in a few days."

"I'm looking forward to seeing them," Lucy said.

We had invited our friends to drop in on Christmas Day and visit with us and Crane's relatives. Hence the baked ham and other buffet-type food. I planned to repeat the menu for New Year's.

"I hope Leonora will be able to make it," I said. "She has the flu or something. She wanted to have a perfect Christmas."

"Let's hope she's back to normal by then. Are you going to Brent's party today?" she added.

"Just for a little while. I'd like to see the new collie he's fostering."

"I suspect he's going to keep her. Brent is like you, Jennet. Adopting all of his rescues."

I took a few more swallows of my tea and prepared it for reading. It seemed that Lucy studied the formations longer than usual. That could be cause for apprehension. Or not.

"I don't see a sleigh," she said. "Is that good or bad?"

"Both," I said. "I'm not eager to see another apparition, but I hate to leave the mystery unsolved."

"You're going to receive many presents and you're going to go to a party."

"At Brent's barn today. The tea leaves are up to date."

"Here's some bad news," Lucy said. "Initial 'V' is still hanging around your home."

Veronica the Viper again, with her sights trained on my husband.

"As long as she stays in the teacup," I said.

"Your wish will be granted." Lucy either began a reading or ended it with the status of my wish. But there was more to come.

"I see a dark cloud over your home," she said and set the cup on the white wicker coffee table.

Those clouds loved to hover over the house on Jonquil Lane, bringing rain or snow or trauma.

"Do you think I have another enemy?" I asked.

"This is more like an unanticipated setback."

"Then it could be something as simple as burning my next batch of cookies."

"That's the spirit," Lucy said.

However, I didn't think it was that simple.

Fifteen

Jingle bells swing and jingle bells ring...

From the moment I stepped into Brent's barn, I heard bells. It took me a moment to realize that his dogs were wearing the kind of jingle bell collars I'd planned on making for my own collies. Maybe the horses were too. They were safely in their stalls, each one of which was decorated with a festive wreath or swag.

Brent had transformed the barn into a winter party place with a towering Christmas tree in its center. Instead of decorating with traditional lights and ornaments, he had decorated the branches with treats for his four-legged friends: dogs, horses, and the indispensable barn cats who kept the area clear of vermin.

Presents for his workers and friends were piled under the tree.

I helped myself to a cup of cider and a handful of cashews from the buffet and looked for Lucy or Annica while Brent's canine crew dashed around, begging for handouts. Nova appeared at my side and thrust her head under my hand wanting to be petted. Brent emerged from the middle of a jolly, boisterous group of young men, no doubt his entire barn crew.

"Hey, Jennet, I see you found the cider," he said. "Would you like something with more punch?"

"

"This is fine."

"Let's find a quiet place. People don't need to hear what we're saying. They'd start asking questions. Outside maybe?"

"It's thirty-seven degrees and snowing outside."

"A little light snow won't hurt you."

"Well, the cold will."

"My office then." He led the way to a small section set apart from the rest of the barn by a half door, then turned to Nova who had followed us. "Come in if you're coming, Nova. If not..."

She jingled her way into the office and, certain of her welcome, made herself at home on a rag rug.

Brent motioned me to a chair but sat on the edge of a cluttered desk. "Alethea came through for me. Faraday Hill, the road, doesn't exist anymore. The house you were looking for was called Faraday Hall. The estate consisted of seventy acres, but it was chopped up years ago. The owners had seven grandchildren. Each of them inherited ten acres."

"What a shame to break up a seventy-acre estate," I said.

"The original house was torn down, and a few of the heirs sold their parcels to a developer. That land became Frost Lake Estates, new home of Alethea Venn."

I hated to give up my idea of the palatial Victorian on the hilltop as the sleigh ride's starting point, but it belonged to somebody else. The land on which the Faraday house had stood would be in another place, unrecognizable and built over.

"Was Alethea curious about the sleigh story?" I asked.

"A little. I told her I didn't have any other details. That's true, right?"

"Just names. They wouldn't mean anything to her."

"That's all I found out. What do you say we join the others?"

"Good idea, since you're the host."

He opened the half door. With a jingle of her bell collar, Nova sprang up to accompany him.

"She's the original velcro dog," he said. "She sticks to me like glue."

Annica came up to us, dressed for a barn party in dark green corduroy pants and a beaded white sweater. Like Nova, she was jingling, courtesy of her silver bell earrings.

"Are you guys keeping secrets from me?" she asked.

"Only background on Faraday Hill," I said.

"Can't I know? I went with you to look for it."

Brent placed his hand on her shoulders and gave her a short summary of what he'd told me.

"We won't find the house then," she said.

"Everything changes over time," Brent pointed out. "Even sleighs. They've been replaced by cars."

"You have one," she said.

"And I only use it on Christmas Eve."

"Look at Brent's Plymouth Belvedere," I said. "Styles change. It's already a dinosaur."

"Hey, don't insult my automobile!"

Apparently losing interest in past times and change, Annica said, "I'm going to hit the buffet. The cookies are Mary Jeanne's contribution. Coming, Jennet?"

"In a while. I want to say hello to Lucy."

She was deep in conversation with Will, who had taken Nova under his wing. They were talking about what a great collie Nova was. Lucy still wore her red dress and had added several gold chains and bangles.

Brent hugged her. "I'm so glad you made it."

"It's not every day I get an invitation to a barn party," she said.

Seeing that we weren't paying attention to her, Nova gave a little yip and sat, offering her paw to anyone inclined to shake hands with her. That person was Jeff.

When Brent strolled over to the buffet to join Annica, Lucy said, "This is a charming party, but I wouldn't stay too long if I were you, Jennet. The roads are terrible."

"I won't," I said. "There's a lot to be said for hosting a party. Let people come to you."

"I wanted to make an appearance for Brent's sake," she added. "Now I've done it."

I looked at my watch. "Let's stay a little longer and leave together."

We agreed to do that, and I went to the window to see how much snow was falling. Nova trotted along at my side. Apparently, she couldn't make up her mind which one of us to be with, Brent or me. Brent's velcro collie indeed.

~ * ~

Snow blanketed the ground and the road beyond and seemed intent on burying my car under a two-inch layer of white. Lucy had been quicker to clear her car, almost as if she'd cast a spell on the snow. Thankful for my high boots, I set about cleaning the windows while heat spread through the interior.

Lucy had just pulled out to the road. We should have driven to the barn together. Or better still, have declined Brent's invitation. Friend or no friend, party or no party, this was the kind of day anyone with a choice stayed home.

Inside, the Ford soon became warm and even toasty. I turned on the windshield wipers and dropped my speed to twenty-five. Fortunately, the car held the road. So far, the surface hadn't gotten slippery yet.

The countryside was rapidly turning white. With no wind to move the snow, it clung to the trees that lined the road. The scenery was breathtaking. If only I could see it more clearly, but falling snow obscured my vision.

But not my hearing. Was that a sound of bells and singing? It carried through the body of the car.

Dashing through the snow,

In a one-horse open sleigh...

I could barely make out the wide verge, thick with snow-encrusted brush, and beyond it, thin woods on ground level with the road. Sensing what was about to happen, I pulled to the side, let the engine run, and waited with the lights on.

Back on the road, a sleigh burst through the wall of snow, its horses moving at a leisurely pace, their bells ringing.

The sleigh with its passengers, their eyes fixed on the road ahead.

They didn't look my way. It was as if I were invisible, an apparition in a strange vehicle.

But I could see them; furthermore, I knew their names: Nicholas, Margaret, Auralee, and Edmund. And somehow, I knew which young man was Nicholas and which was Edmund. Edmund was fair, and Nicholas was dark and very handsome. In the same way I knew that Auralee held a silver necklace that spilled out of her coat, and Margaret held a songbook in her lap.

How odd to trust a book to the elements. Wouldn't it get wet?

Not if it were a spirit's book.

And how very odd to see these details through a veil of snow.

The four riders were in a merry mood, the picture of Christmas joy and camaraderie.

Then they were gone, cut off from my view by the falling snow.

Gone as if they'd been nothing but a dream.

Sixteen

I waited until the sound of sleigh bells faded and finally died. It seemed to take longer than it should. The car was a stable and warm haven in a world that suddenly seemed alien—a world in which time had shifted as it had on Huron Court.

You wanted to see the sleigh again, I reminded myself. *Well, you saw it.*

Would the riders ever reach their home and continue their singing and laughter in front of a roaring fire? Or were they indeed doomed to travel the roads and by-roads of Foxglove Corners forever?

At present, that was unimportant. What mattered was that the sleigh had come and gone and done me no harm. As before, the people—the ghosts—hadn't looked my way.

Curious, though. On both occasions, I was driving alone in a snowstorm on a lonely country road. Were these conditions—snow, lonely road—necessary for me to see the sleigh?

That was a good question. I didn't know the answer yet.

A sudden sadness brought the sting of tears to my eyes as I imagined myself in this situation, riding through the snow with Crane, Brent, and Annica, while life in the real world continued and the years went by. And it was always snowing.

Finally, good sense prevailed. I had to go home, had dogs to care for, dinner to make, and last-minute preparations to see to for guests. And the snow showed no signs of tapering off.

As I drove, I listened for bells, wondering if I would overtake the sleigh farther down the road.

It didn't seem likely, and it didn't happen. By the time I reached Jonquil Lane and my own driveway, the incident had assumed an air of unreality.

Crane wasn't home yet.

Being greeted by eight exuberant collies served to ground me. Dogs, dinner, and a quick tour of the house to make sure everything was ready for our guests. My agenda was a commanding voice, whipping me into action.

For some reason, I felt exhausted, which was unusual for me this early in the afternoon. I went outside with the dogs, counting on cold, fresh air to revive me, then came back inside and stared at the stove hoping for inspiration.

Deciding on spaghetti, I gathered sauce makings and took meatballs out of the freezer. As I worked, the sense of unreality that had gripped me loosened its hold. The apparition was real. I had seen it twice, each time in a different part of Foxglove Corners. I needed to deal with it.

Why? Surely it held particular significance for me.

But what?

I made a cup of hot chocolate and sat in the rocker, sipping it slowly while the sighting replayed itself, and I pulled details from my memory and my imagination.

Auralee was getting cold. She was having fun sleigh riding with her cousin and friends, but she was ready to return to Faraday Hall. She touched her necklace and stole a glance at Nicholas. Time with him was worth a little discomfort. Only her hands were beginning to freeze inside her gloves, and her eyes were watering. She didn't look her best outside, unlike Margaret who was prettier than ever with her dark brown hair and her red coat.

Margaret liked Nicholas, too. A little too much. He appeared to unaware of either of the girls, guiding the horses down the snowy lane as if the sleigh were a ship.

She wondered if it would ever stop snowing.

~ * ~

The snow continued in the real world, my world. Time, real time, passed. A tangy sauce simmered on the stove. The spaghetti was ready to drop in the pot. The salad was in the refrigerator, rolls in the oven. For dessert, always essential, we had half an apple pie.

Crane came in, stamping snow in all directions and dodging collies. He kissed me.

"It's bad out there," he said. "Did you go to Brent's party?"

"For a little while," I said.

I would tell him about the apparition later, after dinner.

"Did you have any trouble?" he asked.

"On the road? No. But I was glad to get home."

"Good. I was worried about you. Too many people were out driving today. I dealt with several accidents, mostly fender benders."

He locked his gun in its cabinet and went upstairs to shower.

While waiting for him to come back down, I called Leonora. She'd asked me to tell her about Brent's party, but I knew from her voice that she was still sick.

"How are you?" I asked.

"I feel terrible," she said. "Camille brought me some chicken soup with her homemade noodles, but all I can have is ginger ale."

"I'm so sorry. Is it the flu?"

"I'm pretty sure, but I had my flu shot."

"I didn't get mine. I meant to, but October was so busy, and by November I forgot about it."

"It's not too late to get one," she said.

"It seems every year I read that the current strain of flu is resistant to the vaccine," I said.

"That's true in my case. I don't know why I bothered getting one."

If I were sick, I would feel the same way. What else could I say? Make the usual offer? "Call if you need anything," I said. "I'll let you rest now."

"Thanks, Jennet, and have a wonderful day with your family."

I ended the call. Leonora had wanted this to be a perfect Christmas. She had two more days to recover. I could only hope that all was not lost.

~ * ~

After dinner, when I told Crane about seeing the sleigh, he said, "I was thinking about you, driving home after Brent's party in all that snow. I kept remembering the last time."

I knew exactly what he was remembering.

"This was different. The roads weren't slippery, and there was no slope to drop down. I just pulled over and waited until it passed by."

"It's funny," he said. "I was thinking about you at the same time you were seeing the sleigh."

"We're on the same wavelength," I said. "And it's not so surprising. You knew I'd be on the road this afternoon."

We had blithely skirted around the significance of the apparition. If it had meaning for me. I thought it did.

"What does Lucy think about this?" he asked.

"We were at the barn together, but she doesn't know about the latest appearance. She said something about the spirits wanting me to help them rest in peace."

"That isn't your responsibility," he said. "It could be dangerous."

"She's only guessing. I want to find out as much as I can about the people."

"Why?"

"I'm curious. Naturally. There's a story there. If I know it, maybe I can stop it."

"How?"

I wilted at his interrogatory tone. "I don't know how. It's just a thought."

"We'll have a full house for Christmas," he said. "You won't be driving alone. That should discourage them."

Discourage spirits from appearing? Was that even possible?

While I didn't imagine they would interact with Crane's family,

I didn't think anything would be powerful enough to keep the sleigh and its occupants away.

He was right, though. I was going to be busy sharing hostess duties with Camille, and I hoped that Christmas would be a ghost-free day. The only time I would be outside would be when I crossed the lane to the yellow Victorian on Christmas Eve. With a little heavenly help, I should be able to outwit the sleigh.

Seventeen

Have yourself a ghostly little Christmas...

My sister, Julia, was the first of our Christmas company to arrive. She had driven down to Foxglove Corners from the little northern town where she was an instructor at a small college.

From the bay window, I watched through a flurry of snow as she unloaded her car, one brightly wrapped package after another, along with a shopping bag decorated with snowmen. What a lot of presents!

Crane went out to help her while the dogs yipped and fussed, first at one door, then the other, waiting for one of them to open.

Julia has always been the essence of sunshine. She can bring light and life to the darkest day. Which wasn't to say that this day before Christmas Eve was particularly dark. On the contrary. With snow blanketing the landscape, it was blindingly white.

I flung open the side door, and she enveloped me in a warm hug so intense that I felt my happy past wrap itself around me like a sun-warmed cloak. Her golden hair spilled out of her red knit hat, and her face glowed in the winter cold.

"Merry Christmas!" she said. Then looking over my shoulder at the horde of excited collies, she added, "Oh, my, the dogs. There are more of them."

"Just one more."

I drew her farther into the kitchen and took her hat and coat while Crane gathered the presents she had brought to set under the tree. The combined brightness of my husband and my sister practically raised the temperature by several degrees.

"Velvet is new," I said. "She's the little tri."

That was how I referred to Velvet when introducing her, as she was black like Halley and Candy, although smaller.

"Velvet?" Julia said.

Ears at attention, Velvet responded to Julia's call and trotted to her side to be petted.

"She *does* feel like velvet," Julia said. "Beautiful black velvet."

Crane came back for another load of presents. "How were the roads?" he asked.

"Not bad. I left early just in case. The house looks great, Jennet."

"Every room has its own special touch of Christmas," I said.

A fresh arrangement of red and white carnations mixed with holly served as a centerpiece on the oak table while my latest batch of cookies sparkled red and green from the crystal server.

"Who would like hot chocolate?" I reached for a large saucepan. Foolish question. All three of us humans. Even the collies looked interested.

"Who all's coming?" Julia asked.

"Aunt Becky, Crane's brother and dad and his cousin, Suanna."

"I never met Suanna," Julia said. "She wasn't at your wedding."

"She's a lovely young woman. You'll like her."

Once, though, before I'd known that Suanna was Crane's cousin, I'd been a little jealous of her. Well, those days were far in the past.

Crane came back for the last of the presents, the contents of the shopping bag. "I had to put the last batch on the credenza, honey," he said. "There's no more room under the tree."

As I stirred the hot chocolate mix, Julia found the mini-marshmallows and my collection of Christmas mugs, freshly washed and set in front of the everyday china. We worked quietly and happily together. Then, Julia said, "Is anything wrong, Jennet? I mean, are you still happy?"

"What strange questions! Why wouldn't I be?"

"It's just that I had a feeling, a premonition, I guess you'd call it. I was so sure something was wrong. Or maybe something is going to be wrong."

I wondered. Could this concern the sleigh? I hadn't planned on mentioning the apparition until after Christmas, if at all, and not to everyone. Julia's premonition didn't come out of left field, though. In some ways, although rarely, she was on that wavelength that Crane and I shared. I didn't believe for one second that the sleigh had made its final appearance.

"Everything's fine," I said. "We're going to have a happy Christmas."

~ * ~

The Ferguson family had traveled to Michigan in two cars. It's almost impossible to caravan across state lines without one driver falling behind. So it was with our company. Crane's brother, Clem, and Aunt Becky were the next to drive up Jonquil Lane. The second car was nowhere in sight.

"Dad and Suanna stopped for a snack in Ohio," Clem said as they stepped out into the swirling snow.

When I first met Crane's Aunt Becky, we had made an instant connection. She was one of those warm and caring people, a true Southern lady, who would mother the whole world if possible. Pretty and elegant, with silver threading through her light brown hair, she had bundled up well for the Michigan weather in a long navy coat and a scarf in addition to a hood.

She was enchanted by the Michigan weather with its abundance of snow. "We're going to have a white Christmas," she announced. "How perfect!"

Clem was an older version of Crane. Nothing else need be said about him.

Once inside, Crane shooed the collies away from the company and took charge of coats and hats and luggage.

Aunt Becky's gaze lingered on the Christmas tree, the undisputed star of the house.

"How beautiful everything is, Jennet. You've created a winter wonderland."

"The snow helps," I said.

"You're staying with us," Crane said. "Dad, Clem, and Suanna are with Camille and Gilbert."

We had one official guest room and a small room with no particular purpose. Crane and I had worked hard to create a second guest room for Julia. She had raved about the poinsettias and the little creche on the dresser and immediately lay on the bed for a nap.

"You must be hungry," Crane added.

"I know I am," Clem said. "We decided to drive through without stopping."

"How does Jennet's roast beef sound?"

"Wonderful," Aunt Becky said.

"We waited for you. I'll call Julia."

I checked on my dinner, then the dining room table, already set with places for Crane's dad and cousin, and lit the red tapers in our heirloom candlesticks. Aunt Becky had given them to us on our wedding day 'to bring a blessing on your home,' she'd said.

I stepped back to admire the table one last time before calling the diners. Candlelight shone on the table with its china, silver, and crystal, the best we could offer for Christmas. Family and history, peace and goodwill, and the American dream—those were the blessings the candlesticks brought.

~ * ~

Late that evening, I watched from the second story bedroom as the last of our Christmas guests arrived. Crane's dad and Suanna, the ones who had fallen behind for a snack, went straight to the yellow Victorian where it seemed that every lamp Camille owned was lit.

Crane, who had been waiting for them, crossed the lane. He rapped on the door. It opened, and he vanished inside.

The snow had stopped falling and, as yet, nothing disturbed the white-draped vista except tire tracks and boot prints. For once, the winds were still, leaving the snow where it had fallen, clinging to trees and low-growing vegetation.

Here was another Christmas card scene, the view from my window. It seemed to have come together especially for me.

I heard it then, a faint far-off jingle of bells.

Sleigh bells...Clear, merry bells...Their music carried to my window on the still air. It seemed that every woodland creature, every deer, every coyote, even the night birds, wore jingle bell collars and were on the move.

I held my breath. Waited. And waited.

Far down on the snowy lane, the phantom sleigh glided into view.

Eighteen

The bells were loud. So loud. Louder than sleigh bells should be. If they were normal sleigh bells, that is. Which they weren't.

Misty padded over to the window and placed her paws on the sill, wanting to see what I was looking at. She gave a little whimper.

Company coming?

She saw the sleigh. Misty, my psychic collie, was as aware of the strange vehicle from the other world as I was.

Which meant she could she hear the bells, too. Certainly they were loud enough to wake the dead.

Aunt Becky and Julia were sleeping across the hall. They had gone to bed early, exhausted from their long drives. But who could sleep through this unholy clamor? Any minute I expected one of them to wake and want to know what was happening.

And what of Camille, Gilbert, the newly-arrived company, and Crane across the lane in the yellow Victorian? How could they not hear the earsplitting ringing of the sleigh bells? Why weren't they streaming out to the porch to investigate?

I let my hand rest on Misty's ruff, drawing comfort from her warmth. Halley joined us, pressing close to my other side. I gave her a pat, too, grateful to be so well-guarded and blessed.

I sent up a silent prayer. *Please, let the sleigh move quickly up the lane and out of my life.*

But it didn't. In fact, the sleigh had ceased to move. It looked like an oversized Christmas decoration set in the middle of the snowy lane, the horses as still as life-sized statues. Through a gentle fall of snow, I saw the four riders. Auralee, Nicholas, Margaret, and Edmund. They were singing, the music of the sweet carol muted by the clanging bells.

Now the holly bears the berry as white as the milk,
And Mary bore Jesus who was wrapped up in silk...

How long I stayed at the window I couldn't tell. Five minutes? Fifteen? Gradually I became aware that I was shivering in my long flannel nightgown, separated from the cold night by only a single pane of glass.

I no longer saw the sleigh. It hadn't moved on; it had simply ceased to be. All I was looking at was falling snow, and a landscape buried in pristine white and steeped in stillness.

Crane would be coming back from the yellow Victorian soon, and I'd have a chance to talk to him in private. I crawled into bed and pulled the covers up to my chin, which was the dogs' signal to return to their own sleeping places in the doorway. Thank heavens for flannel sheets and warm blankets.

Somewhat relaxed and definitely warmer, I pondered the significance of the apparition. Very little time had elapsed between appearances, and this third one was different in particularly frightening ways. First, it had materialized in front of my own house. Then, for a brief time—how long?—it had been stationary, although the singers hadn't stopped their song and the bells still rang.

How could I doubt that the apparition was meant for me alone?

Here was something else to think about. Didn't the prancing motion of a sleigh's horses cause the bells to ring? That only made sense, but the sleigh moved in a Twilight Zone world. Bells rang even when the sleigh stood still. *Were* there any rules?

Fear threaded its way through my thoughts. Where would the sleigh be when it next appeared? In my own driveway? For at this point, I didn't doubt I would see it again.

Unable to answer my own questions, I closed my eyes. Not to sleep. To wait for Crane and, while waiting, to think about the people who had been so close to my front door. As close as wassail singers of old.

~ * ~

Margaret loved the cold and the feel of the snow on her face. She longed to push back her hood and let the snow land on her hair. Lightly, sweetly, each drop a precious white jewel falling from the sky.

But that wouldn't be proper, and she was, above all, a lady. Also, it wouldn't be healthy. She might catch her death of cold.

Edmund whispered something to her, perhaps a compliment or an endearment, half heard over the ringing of the bells. She gave him a smile in return. It didn't matter what he said.

Under the blanket that covered their legs, he reached for her hand.

Tomorrow would be Christmas day. She had a special gift for Nicholas, one she'd made herself. Shaking the ends of her scarf to dislodge the snow, she smiled to think of him unwrapping it. He'd be sure to love it and be impressed with her skill. Possibly he would look at her in a different way.

Christmas was a time of miracles. She could hope that God had set aside one for her.

~ * ~

I woke when Crane stepped over Halley and stumbled over a squeak toy as he walked to the bed. "Sorry honey," he whispered. "I tried to be quiet."

I turned on the lamp on the nightstand. "It's all right. I have to talk to you."

He sat on the edge of the bed. "What's the matter?"

"Did you hear anything unusual tonight?"

"No. Did you?"

His face told me he knew the answer.

"The sleigh came back," I said. "The bells were so loud they must have heard them all the way up and down the lane."

The ghost bells that only I could hear.

"None of us heard anything. Did it drive by the house?"

"It parked in front of it for a while."

I glanced at the bedside clock. It was ten-thirty. I had slept without dreaming for over an hour.

I said, "Misty and I watched it. The riders were singing, but the bells were so loud you could barely hear them." I paused. I knew the answer but I had to ask. "Was I the only one who heard it?" I didn't want to think that was the case. Fear is more easily managed when it's shared.

"As far as we know, yes," Crane said. "Then what happened?"

"It disappeared."

"The horses didn't pull it away?"

I forced my mind back to that moment. "No, it just vanished. One minute I was looking at the sleigh. The next, I was watching snow falling. I don't suppose you saw any tracks in the lane?"

"Just my boot prints," he said. "With other people around, I hoped this phenomenon or whatever it is would stay away."

"Aunt Becky and Julia must have slept through it," I said. "I'll ask them in the morning."

Crane turned off the light and got into bed beside me. "We need help, Jennet."

Not 'you need help' but '*we* need help'.

Didn't I say we were on the same wavelength, Crane and I?

"Lucy's coming for Christmas," I said. "She may have some idea of what we can do."

~ * ~

Things, I believed, were always better in the morning. No matter how dire they seemed, the new day brought a chance to view them in a different light. It came with new coping mechanisms.

That belief was hard to hold onto when I bundled up, called to Misty, and tramped through the snow to look for sleigh tracks on the lane.

They weren't there.

I'd hoped to see evidence that a real sleigh had halted in front of the house, however unlikely that was.

My fears from the previous night came bouncing back, a demented boomerang.

I imagined a scenario in which the riders climbed out of the sleigh and marched up to the front door, demanding entrance. Auralee, Nicholas, Margaret, and Edmund. Except they wouldn't march; they'd glide. They were, after all, spirits.

Only Misty would bark at them because the other collies wouldn't be aware of their presence. What would happen then? I was afraid to let the scene continue.

"Why are you haunting me?" I said the words aloud. "What did I do wrong?"

Mmm. Many things in my life, but I couldn't think of anything that would merit this unholy visitation.

Well, I had company and breakfast to cook. Inside, I found Julia sitting at the oak table drinking coffee. I assumed Aunt Becky was still sleeping. Misty shook her coat free of snow and left us in search of a post-breakfast napping spot, trailing clumps of snow in her wake.

Julia hid a yawn. "What were you doing outside so early?"

"Checking the lane. Did you sleep well?"

"Pretty well, but all night I dreamed about bells ringing. Do you have a new clock?"

"No, just the ones we've always had." I sat forward. Could Julia have heard the ghost bells?

"It was a nice dream," she added. "I was in a sleigh. Don't you wish we could go for a sleigh ride?"

"Not really, but there are local farmers who offer them, if that's what you want to do." I let the matter drop. "I'm afraid I have a new mystery."

She set her cup on the table. "You assured me that everything was all right. Is that awful woman chasing Crane again?"

"Veronica? I hope not."

"Because if she is, I'll help you get rid of her for good."

"How?"

"Give me time to think of a way. Tell me about the mystery."

"It started with the sound of sleigh bells," I said, and took her back with me to that harrowing night on Windemere Road.

When I finished with a description of last night's sighting, she said, "That is *so* weird. It's like a story being played out for your benefit. I get why you're spooked. These ghosts are stalking you."

"In a way."

But it was true. They had showed themselves to me, so far in three different locations...where I happened to be. In this last instance, in front of the place where I lived.

"And to think I slept through it," she said. "The next time the sleigh shows up, call me, no matter what else is going on."

"I will."

Even though I knew full well that in all probability Julia wouldn't see a thing.

But wait! Last night she had heard sleigh bells ringing. Did that mean she might eventually experience the phenomenon? If so, we'd be two against four, which weren't exactly encouraging odds. But at least I wouldn't be taking on the phantom sleigh alone.

Nineteen

Julia poured another cup of coffee for herself and one for me. The first few sips banished the cold that had taken possession of me.

"I made pancakes for Crane," I said. "Would you like some?"

"Just coffee's okay for now." She pushed back a strand of wayward golden hair. "Let's wait for Becky."

I'd only had toast with Crane, planning on cooking another breakfast for Julia and Aunt Becky. Now that Julia knew about the apparition, I felt less apprehensive, more like tucking into a stack of pancakes drenched in maple syrup.

Let come what may.

"I've been thinking," Julia said. "We'll be like the girl detectives in those old series books you collect. How does this sound? *The Greenway Girls and the Mysterious Sleigh.*"

"Yes!" I could picture an old-time volume with our images on the cover and a sleigh in the background. The notion, while fantastical, pushed my fear factor down to a respectable level.

"I'm counting on a brief respite because of Christmastime," I said.

"Ah yes, the time when *no spirit dare stir abroad.*"

I smiled. *"Nor fairy takes, nor witch hath power to charm/ So hallowed and so gracious is the time.*

We both loved the speech from *Hamlet* and, even more, liked exchanging literary quotes.

"Do you believe it's true?" Julia asked.

"I hope so."

Candy peered into the kitchen. Not seeing one of her favorite foods cooking on the griddle, she lay down, crossed her paws, and waited for a more satisfying view.

I went back to my coffee and my thoughts. If these nights were indeed wholesome, I didn't have to worry about seeing the sleigh and riders for two days. On the other hand, according to the account of the disappearance, the sleigh ride took place on Christmas Eve. Did the sleigh appear on the anniversary of the original ride? If so, could I expect to see it on the lane again tonight?

The nights are wholesome then, I told myself. *No spirit dare stir abroad.*

"Becky and Suanna would like to go Christmas shopping this morning," Julia said. "We could take them to the Maplebrook Mall, but I thought the Green House of Antiques would be more fun. What do you think?"

"That it's a good idea. I know they'll be open for the last-minute shoppers. Afterward, we can have a light lunch at Clovers. They're closing early for the holidays, but we should be able to do both."

Camille's family dinner was this evening. Hence the light lunch.

"Maybe I can find a book for my collection at the Green House," I said.

I already owned several series, and they all needed additions, especially the Beverly Grays.

I heard footsteps upstairs. Aunt Becky was awake. Now for a nice pancake breakfast, and we could officially begin our day.

~ * ~

Crane's cousin, Suanna, was a slender, black-haired beauty with the gray eyes that ran in the Ferguson family. She was bundled up in layers and a green down coat with a hood. I thought she'd be comfortable at the North Pole. Like Aunt Becky, she marveled at the snow that covered the landscape.

They piled into the car, and I drove out to the lane, watching for patches of ice.

"You ladies are going to love the Green House of Antiques," Julia said. "They have bona fide antiques and reproductions and all sorts of unusual gifts. I'd much rather shop there than at a mall where everything is pretty bland."

"I'd love to look at antique jewelry," Suanna said.

She shared Annica's love for unique earrings. I'd noticed her crystal snowflake eardrops sparkling through waves of raven hair.

"They have a wonderful selection," I said.

"Something Christmasy," she added and broke off. "Oh, what a gorgeous house!"

I slowed as we approached the white Queen Anne Victorian, without a doubt the largest and fanciest house on Jonquil Lane. It was for sale—again. The mansion had changed hands several times since I'd moved to Foxglove Corners. I suspected it was too expensive to maintain, not to mention its out-of-this-world asking price.

"It looks like a wedding cake," Aunt Becky said.

"Camille and I explored the interior while it was being built," I said. "It's lovely inside, too."

At present, of course, it was empty, and no one had cleared the long winding walkway yet. The realtor should have done that and perhaps hung a wreath on the door.

"It looks haunted," Suanna said.

Her observation surprised me. "Why do you say that?"

"It seems so sad and lonely, as if it were a happy place once, and knows it'll never be like that again."

"Interesting."

I would have described the Queen Anne Victorian as one more Foxglove Corners Christmas card scene, but to each his own. Strange that Suanna had that impression. Strange but in a good way. In my view, with her affinity for the exquisite Victorian, she had just demonstrated that she was one of us.

~ * ~

Of all the shops on the street known as Antique Row, the Green House had the best window displays, and whatever the season, the owner always made good use of books. On a ground covered with imitation snow, a pathway made of childhood classics, most with a holiday slant, led to a Santa's castle in which a life-sized figure of Santa himself sat on a gold throne.

Julia opened the door to the shop, and I started at the ringing of sleigh bell—before I reminded myself that they were a common enough decoration at this time of year. She, Aunt Becky, and Suanna went inside while I took a few minutes to admire the display. Tiny elves danced around the books while old-fashioned story book dolls, arranged in a semi-circle, looked on.

And the books! *A Christmas Carol, The Polar Express, The Little Fir Tree and Other Stories, The Christmas Collie,* a pristine edition of a vintage Judy Bolton, *The Secret of the Musical Tree...*

Those who knew me knew that I considered a book the best present of all. And since I was here in my favorite store, I was going to buy one for myself. I told myself I deserved it and set the bells ringing again as I followed the others into the Green House.

The crowded store greeted its customers with splashes of red and green. "The Little Drummer Boy" played softly in the background while the sleigh bells rang whenever anyone entered the shop or left it, burdened with packages.

My companions had separated, each following her own interest. Suanna had found the antique jewelry, and Julia was examining frilly vintage blouses. Aunt Becky lingered at a table set with china in a holly berry and candy cane pattern.

I wound my way through the aisles, knowing that the books were scattered throughout the shop, resting on tables, desks, and glass-fronted bookcases.

The X Bar X Boys Lost in the Rockies lay open, its yellowing pages illuminated by a delicate Tiffany style lamp. It wasn't a series I collected, but stories set in the old West held a special place in my heart. On a nearby table, I found something more appealing: *The Adventure Girls at K Bar O* and *Spurs for Antonia.*

Then a small oil painting caught my attention. Did I say caught? It practically leaped off the wall into my arms. Framed in scallop-edged dark wood, it depicted a glistening snow scene, the focal point of which was a horse-drawn sleigh traveling on a narrow tree-bordered lane.

I stared at it, mesmerized.

It was *the* sleigh. My sleigh.

Twenty

It can't be, I thought.

How could a supernatural manifestation—*my* apparition—appear in a painting for sale at the Green House of Antiques?

It simply couldn't be, but it was, undeniably so, a likeness of the phantom sleigh and its occupants.

I told myself that horse-drawn sleighs were a popular subject for winter art, especially at Christmas. Except this sleigh was like none other. It held two couples. One of the women wore a red coat, the other a green scarf. The man who guided the horses was incredibly handsome; his companion was attractive enough, but not so striking. They were Auralee, Nicholas, Margaret, and Edmund, immortalized in oil. Exactly as I'd seen them.

The strangest detail, though, was the collie, the Lassie dog, who ran with the sleigh. She was a mirror image of Nova.

She might have been part of the sleigh riding company, however, before they became an apparition. Then, as dogs sometime do, she had detached herself from it. Curious, though, that I'd only seen her once, on that first sighting.

Explain that.

Later, when I'd had ample time to reflect.

The artist's signature, G. Allemand, was written in a snowdrift. Knowing who had painted the haunting scene was important if I hoped to trace it; and I did. Providence had handed me my first clue, and I might never have seen it if we hadn't gone shopping at the Green House.

Julia joined me, carrying two blouses. "Help me decide," she said. Then she saw the painting. "Jennet, it's the sleigh! Just the way you described it."

"You see it, too?"

"Red coat, green scarf, handsome man. What else could it be? But how could someone paint an apparition?"

I voiced the first idea that came to me. "Somebody else must have seen the phantom sleigh and was so enchanted by the sight they created it in oil."

"That could be. You have to buy it," she added.

"I'm going to. I don't see a price tag."

For this treasure, price wasn't a factor. I lifted the painting down from the wall, for some reason expecting it to be warm, but it was cold, as cold as it would be if it had been lying in snow.

"I suppose four young people disappearing without a trace gave rise to stories and maybe inspired drawings and this painting," I said.

"That makes sense. Then over the years, the tale faded, and finally died a natural death."

"Remember, the country was about to enter World War Two. That fact probably hastened its death."

Since my companions were still engrossed in their shopping, I had time to look for my book. Instead of taking the painting to the cash register, I held on to it. In case Fate decided to snatch it out of my hands.

~ * ~

We spent over an hour at the Green House of Antiques, buying presents for others and for ourselves. I was happy to know I wasn't the only one who purchased a gift for herself.

"So we can have something from Santa," Aunt Becky said. She had found a holly and ivy patterned tablecloth similar to the one that covered the store's table set for an imaginary dinner.

Julia bought a lacy white blouse to wear with her green velvet skirt, and Suanna added three pairs of earrings to her collection. The other gifts, wrapped by the clerk, were destined to join the many packages already under the tree.

"Let's stop at Clovers for a quick lunch," I said, although there was no need to hurry.

"I *am* hungry," Julia said.

I hoped Annica was working. I couldn't wait to show her the painting.

~ * ~

Annica was there, dressed like a candy cane in a red jumper and white blouse. She was filling the dessert carousel with holiday-frosted cakes. Wherever you looked in the little restaurant, you saw the happy color, red, in the poinsettia plants and crimson ornaments that adorned the miniature tree centerpieces.

"How pretty," Suanna said. "You have the nicest places in Foxglove Corners, Jennet."

I introduced Suanna to Annica, but Aunt Becky remembered Annica from the wedding. My favorite booth was free, and we made ourselves comfortable, removing coats, gloves, and scarves.

"What's good for lunch?" I asked.

"We have an abbreviated menu because we're closing early," Annica said. "But we have good pea soup and country ham sandwiches, and for dessert, a lot of wonderful things. I decorated the cakes."

"Before we order, I want to show you what I found at the Green House of Antiques." I pulled the painting out of the shopping bag.

"It's charming," Annica said. "Wait! Isn't that...?"

She broke off with a glance at me, no doubt realizing that I hadn't told everyone about the phantom sleigh.

Quickly I said, "Yes, it's perfect for a Christmas gift from me to me. I'm going to keep it out all year."

Aunt Becky and Suanna exclaimed over it, and Suanna pointed out that the snow on the canvas glistened like the real snow outside. It was as if the painting were sprinkled with glitter.

"The people look so real they could almost step out of the canvas," Aunt Becky said.

I was at a loss for words, having imagined that very scenario: Nicholas bringing the horses to a halt and Edmund helping Margaret down from the sleigh. Julia stepped in to save the day.

"If the people came to life, they're so tiny they'd be in danger of getting stepped on."

Suanna laughed. "Like fairy folk."

Annica said, "As soon as Clovers closes, I'm going Christmas shopping. Oh, by the way, Marcy and I get to take home the desserts that didn't sell."

"Now *that's* a Christmas gift," Aunt Becky said.

Annica jotted down our orders and took a last look at the painting before I set it back in the shopping bag.

"I love your snow scene, Jennet," she said, "but isn't it an amazing coincidence that you found it?"

Suanna and Aunt Becky looked puzzled, but Annica had left before they could question her. I decided to tell them the story behind the painting and my part in it soon. I suspected that Aunt Becky, at least, would be receptive to the supernatural aspect of the incidents, for she had once seen the ghost of a Confederate soldier who haunted a ruined Tennessee garden.

But I wouldn't tell them yet. And not here in a public place.

~ * ~

When we reached home, Aunt Becky crossed the lane to help Camille with dinner, and Julia set out for a short walk. I unlocked the side door, and we were immediately set upon by the excited collie pack. I started to shoo them away from Suanna, but she stopped me, laughing as they pranced and danced around her feet.

"I love dogs, and these are so beautiful. They're all different colors. I don't know which one to pet first."

The collies had their own ideas:

Me...me...me...me...me...Choose me. No, me! Candy jumped up on Suanna, her company manners flying out the window.

"Candy, no!" I grabbed her collar, and Suanna held on to the edge of the table to keep from falling.

"Sorry," I said. "Candy is a wild one. Velvet is new. Raven is the bi-black. This is Star. Misty..." I finished the introductions, making sure that everyone had the attention she craved.

"How did you get so many?" she asked.

"I belong to a collie rescue organization. Halley is the only dog I purchased. The others were rescues." As Halley had stationed herself closest to me, I gave her an extra pat.

"They're the most beautiful dogs I've ever seen," Suanna said.

"Thank you. I think so."

It was probably too soon to tell Suanna about Misty's sixth sense, but I could give her a short biography of each dog. Anyone who appreciates my collies wins a special and immediate place in my heart. Once again, Suanna had demonstrated that she was one of us.

Twenty-one

A light snow began to fall as Julia, Suanna, and I walked across the lane to the yellow Victorian. We bore gifts. Suanna carried the presents she'd purchased at the Green House, and Julia and I each had a tin of my home-baked Christmas cookies.

"This is my first real white Christmas," Suanna said. "I *love* the snow."

She kicked at a snowdrift and sent glistening white particles flying into the air.

"Last Christmas we had a blizzard," I said. "Everyone spent the night with us, even Camille and Gilbert. That's how deep the snow was."

"I wouldn't like that," Suanna said.

"You wouldn't think so, but it was fun," Julia assured her.

"And we had a holiday haunting." I was paving the way for the sleigh story which I planned to tell the Southern branch of the family after dinner.

Julia said, "You kept hearing bells then too, didn't you, Jennet?"

I hadn't forgotten. "Our ghost was a collie named Macduff who was looking for the family that abandoned him."

"How terribly sad. But you called him a ghost?"

"He was only there in spirit."

"Jennet's ghosts are almost always collies," Julia said. "I wonder why that is."

"Julia is exaggerating." I added, "Macduff's story had a happy ending. He left, and we're pretty sure he found his peace."

At the other end of the lane, the going was easier as Gilbert had cleared the walkway. Camille had decorated lavishly with candles in all the windows, mostly the safe kind that looked as if they were burning but ran on battery power. From inside, Twister, the Belgian shepherd, and Holly, the black collie, were barking and the strains of a beloved old carol drifted out into the cold air:

I wonder as I wander out under the sky

How Jesus our savior was born for to die...

I came close to stumbling over a toy left on the porch when a familiar sound in the distance insinuated its way through the mournful strains.

Sleigh bells.

You don't hear them, I told myself. *It's Christmas Eve. No spirit dare stir abroad.*

The bells continued to ring.

The front door was ajar, most likely an oversight as the air was frigid. Still, I rapped lightly.

Gilbert invited us in. He looked dapper in a red reindeer sweater. "Merry Christmas! Come in out of the cold." He took Suanna's packages and the cookie tins and set them on a table in the hall.

I breathed in the scents that defined Christmas for me—fresh balsam and roasting turkey. Gilbert took our coats, and we gravitated toward the tree which they'd set up near the fireplace. It was magnificent, loaded with vintage ornaments and strings of lights that resembled burning candles.

I caught a glimpse of Camille's table in the dining room, all white and silver with frosted evergreen branches in crystal vases. It reminded me of an illustration in *Pure Michigan.*

"Where is everyone?" Julia asked.

"The guys are in the kitchen, sampling dinner," Gilbert said. "Becky is putting together a relish tray."

Camille appeared, her 'Come woo me' apron protecting her green dress from various spills. "Merry Christmas, girls. You all look so pretty."

"What can we do to help?" I asked.

"Not a thing. Everything's done. We'll just wait for Crane."

"He'll be along in a few minutes," I said. "I'm so glad he could join us. Crime is taking a break for the holiday."

Along with supernatural manifestations. Or so I hoped.

~ * ~

Before we sat down to dinner, Crane took me aside. "I saw your new painting, Jennet. It's a picture of the haunted sleigh, isn't it? With the four people? I mean, the ghosts?"

"It has to be."

"Where did it come from?"

"The Green House of Antiques. The artist signed it. After Christmas, I'm going to try to find some information on him."

"I don't like having it in the house," he said.

I looked at him. He was serious. Even troubled.

"Why?" I asked.

"It's bad luck."

That sentiment was unlike anything Crane would normally say. I wondered. Could he be right? Was I, in essence, inviting the apparition into our home?

"We don't have to keep it," I said. "We won't, if it bothers you. I'll give it to Lucy. She'll love it and probably use it in her next book."

"Do *you* want to keep it?" he asked.

"Not necessarily. I thought it might help me understand what's going on with the sleigh."

"What are you two whispering about?" Camille asked. "Everybody—we're ready."

Gilbert brought in the turkey platter, pretending it was too heavy for him. While Crane and I had been talking about the painting, Aunt Becky and Julia had carried in bowls of rice, stuffing, cranberries, Brussels sprouts and assorted trimmings.

"What a feast!" Crane's father took the bowl of stuffing Camille offered him.

"Well, it's Christmas." Camille touched her locket. Obviously a Christmas present, obviously edged in diamonds.

"It's wonderful to have all the handsome Ferguson men together at one table," Aunt Becky said. "Just like old times. Oh, and you too, Suanna dear, of course."

Clem sat opposite me, and I again marveled at his close resemblance to Crane. This is what Crane would look like in seven years. In thirty years, he would resemble his father.

I was blessed to be part of this family. Even though Rebecca Ferguson's candlesticks were at home on our credenza, I imagined her looking down on us and smiling. No evil thing would have its way with us while Rebecca watched over her descendants and their wives.

~ * ~

After dinner, after we'd unwrapped our gifts and were having coffee and finishing the Yule log, I said to no one in particular, "We live in an unusual little town. Foxglove Corners has a reputation for welcoming ghosts."

"Ghosts?" Suanna said. "Who believes in ghosts?"

Her question surprised me, as she had appeared to accept my story about the ghost dog, Macduff.

Crane gave her a fond smile. "People who live in Foxglove Corners, Cousin."

"I do," Aunt Becky said. "I saw a ghost once."

"Really, Aunt?" Clem looked surprised. "I thought that was just a story you made up for us kids."

"It was all true. I saw him as clearly as I see any of you around this table. He came home after the war to find his house and garden in ruins and his family gone. He never moved on."

She had given me the opening I needed.

"I'm a believer, too," I said. "A few weeks ago, I was almost run off the road by a phantom sleigh." I told them the story of the hauntings, and all of the fear I had known on that snowy night came back as strong as ever.

Suanna said, "Seriously?"

"Seriously. I saw it more than once. The last time, it parked in front of our house."

I could tell she didn't believe me but was too polite to say so.

I said, "At the time, before World War Two, four young people went for a sleigh ride and never came home. Their story is one of Foxglove Corner's most enduring mysteries."

"Where did they go?" Suanna asked.

"Nobody knows. Their bodies were never found. Neither was the sleigh."

"But *you* saw this sleigh?

"And the people. I should say their spirits. They looked like they did when they were young." Based on Suanna's reaction to my tale, I didn't add their names and the little I'd deduced about them.

Crane covered my hand with his own. "There are so many ghosts floating around Foxglove Corners, it's hard to avoid them. Just think, Suanna. You may see one, too."

"I'd die if that happened," she said.

Twenty-two

I woke the next morning to the sound of sleigh bells ringing. The phantom sleigh was near. Coming down the lane?

Dear God, I hoped not.

I swung out of bed and hurried to the window.

The new layer of snow glistened on the ground, blown into marshmallow white swirls. The lane was empty. And the bells? I listened. I could barely hear them now, but they were still there, either farther up or down the lane, still too close for comfort.

"Find another lane to haunt," I said. "And stay there."

Misty looked up at me as if to ask if I were talking to her.

"Not you, girl."

I heard Crane moving downstairs and the scampering of collie nails on the kitchen floor. He was going to let the dogs out. Misty followed Halley down the stairs. I slipped on my long white robe and followed them.

I would let Julia and Aunt Becky sleep and save these first precious moments of Christmas morning for Crane and me.

Having arrived in the kitchen too late to join the other collies, Halley and Misty began to whine. I opened the kitchen door and let them out, then wandered through the house.

Crane had plugged in the tree lights. They filled the living room with a soft, ethereal glow. He'd also built a fire. The sleigh painting lay on the credenza where I'd left it. I turned it face down on the white crocheted scarf.

"You're not welcome in this house today," I said. "Or ever."

There's no call for fear, I told myself. *You have it all. Snow, a home, firelight, family, and the finest collies in the land to protect you from evil.*

But I couldn't quite banish the apprehension that gripped me.

I had set the table for breakfast last night before going to bed. On my plate I found the two green packages I'd seen under the tree. Crane's gifts to me. Or, as he'd say, from Santa to me. My presents for him were under the tree.

I lifted one of the boxes and shook it. Jewelry, I was pretty sure, next to books, my favorite gift.

I plugged in the coffeemaker and began mixing pancake batter. How to make this breakfast extra special when I tried hard to make every breakfast memorable for Crane? Grapefruit, I decided, with cherries in the center.

They came in, eight collies and one man, all of them leaving gobs of snow on the doormat.

"Merry Christmas, honey." Crane's kiss came with a sprinkling of snow that had attached itself to his jacket sleeve and a lot of cold air. But I didn't care. I wished him a Merry Christmas and returned his kiss with interest.

"Aren't you going to open your presents from Santa?" he asked.

I was happy to let breakfast slide and do as he said. Opening the larger box, I found a lovely emerald and crystal bracelet.

"Oh, how beautiful!" I opened the other. Wrapped in tissue was a pair of matching earrings. "Beyond beautiful," I finished.

"Like you." He clasped the bracelet on my wrist, and I admired it in the first of the morning light.

"I'll wear the earrings when I get dressed," I said.

I was going to wear my green dress. The stones would bring out the green in my eyes. No one knew me better than Crane; no one knew better what to say to make me happy.

"I'll get breakfast moving along," I said.

Julia and Aunt Becky came downstairs together.

"What smells so good?" Aunt Becky asked.

"Pancakes and bacon," I said.

"And coffee." Julia poured cups of coffee for herself and Aunt Becky. "I see Santa brought you a new bracelet, Jennet. It's exquisite."

I held my arm out for her to see it better. "That's Santa Crane. We'll open presents after breakfast, but these two couldn't wait."

Before long the pancakes were ready. We sat around the oak table, the collies lying as close to us as they dared. With four people, handouts were guaranteed. Crane had slipped a CD of Christmas carols into the player.

From time to time as I ate, I glanced at my bracelet and felt the magic of Christmas take hold of the entire house.

The only bells I heard came from the CD player.

~ * ~

Julia and I set up a buffet in the dining room: The ham on a platter with plenty of slices already carved, potato salad, relishes, rolls and bread. Fruitcakes and other desserts covered the credenza, and I took pleasure in moving the sleigh painting to a drawer. Its day would come.

Roughly half of the gifts had been opened, and other half waited in brightly wrapped packages for their recipients. A little after noon it started to snow again, large fluffy flakes that added another layer to the landscape and more Christmas atmosphere.

Brent was the first of our guests to arrive. He brought Lucy and Annica with him and, surprisingly, the collie Nova.

"I knew you wouldn't mind having another dog around, Jennet," he said. "Something came up. It concerns Nova, and I didn't want to leave her alone at home or even at the barn. There's only one man there today."

I took the presents he carried, and Julia took Nova's leash. "How about a nice drink of water, Nova?" she asked.

"Of course I don't mind," I said, "but what came up? You sound worried."

He lowered his voice. "Tell you later. Is that a whole ham I see?"

"It is. You all can help yourselves.

"Later," Lucy said. "Annica and I just had breakfast."

"Were you out celebrating on Christmas Eve?" I asked.

"In a way," Annica said. "We went with Brent to deliver presents."

I knew about Brent's tradition. Every year he bought toys and clothes for needy children in Foxglove Corners. It was a spectacular production. He dressed in a Santa Claus suit, loaded his sleigh, and visited each house to deliver them.

His sleigh! Maybe that was the sleigh I heard last night and early this morning.

"Do you have bells on your sleigh?" I asked.

"On the horses. Why?" Enlightenment dawned before I could answer him. "As far as I know, mine was the only sleigh in Foxglove Corners last night," he said.

As far as he knew. Brent wouldn't have seen the sleigh. It was my apparition, and it was high time to set it on the back burner for the rest of the holiday.

~ * ~

They trooped through the lightly falling snow across the lane and stood on the porch—Camille and Gilbert, Clem and Suanna.

We opened the rest of the presents, ate ham sandwiches, and munched on cookies, then gathered in small groups. Julia and Suanna found *It's a Wonderful Life* on television and were soon engrossed in it. Some movies never grow old.

I was in the kitchen replenishing the relish tray when Brent caught up with me.

"That matter with Nova," he said. "Here's what happened. Some guy tracked me down at the barn yesterday. He claims Nova belongs to him. She was surrendered by mistake."

"Who makes that kind of mistake?"

"His wife. It turns out she didn't want Nova but changed her mind. That's all he would tell me."

"I don't understand. What shelter reveals the name of a person who adopts one of their dogs?"

"They don't. He wouldn't say how he found me."

"You're not going to give her to him, I hope."

"Damn right. Sorry. Lucy says no swearing on Christmas Day."

"How did you leave it with him?" I asked.

"He said if I didn't let him take her, he was going to get a court order and come back for her."

"He can't do that. It's a scare tactic."

"That's why I brought her here today. I wouldn't put it past him to do something underhanded."

"He sounds like a bully."

"He doesn't know who he's dealing with," Brent said.

Twenty-three

As Christmas night wound down, I remembered the sleigh painting I intended to give to Lucy. I called her over to the credenza and opened the drawer. There they were, the ghostly revelers, frozen in place but looking as if they were ready to leap off the canvas. It was as if they resented being shut away from the merriment.

Ridiculous. Nevertheless, I became aware of a fleeting sense of fear, fueled largely by my runaway imagination.

"This looks like your apparition," Lucy said.

"Exactly like it. Crane thinks it's bad luck for us to keep it. I want you to have it. Oh—I don't mean I want to transfer my bad luck to you."

She laughed. "I didn't take it that way. It's a beautiful snow scene. I'd love to have it."

"I found it in the Green House of Antiques," I said. "I thought you could use it in a story."

"I can see many possibilities. Thank you."

Lucy touched the canvas, her hand lingering on the drifted snow. "How real this looks. You almost expect it to feel cold and wet. What an amazing artist."

"Do you think someone else saw the sleigh and painted it from memory?"

"Maybe, but it could also be that the artist knew the people involved and captured their story on canvas."

I hadn't considered that. It was worth pursuing.

"In real life, the girls were Auralee and Margaret Faraday," I said. "They were cousins. The dark, handsome man was Nicholas. The other was Edmund. I learned that from the real-life account, but somehow I already knew their names and knew that both girls were interested in Nicholas. Don't ask me how."

Lucy was silent for a moment. I thought she might suggest how I came by that knowledge, but all she said was, "It's good to know the names of the spirits that haunt you."

Brent sauntered up to the credenza, a glass of eggnog in his hand. Nova stood at his side, wagging her tail. She had stayed close to him all evening. "Another present, Lucy? You made out like a bandit this year."

"This is a depiction in oil of what Jennet saw. I'm going to keep it for her."

"How could anyone...? Oh, I see. Those sleigh riding ghosts are showing themselves to other people."

"We don't know, but I'm going to do more research," I said.

After Aunt Becky and company left for Tennessee, I planned to head to the library. Julia was staying until after New Year's. I knew she'd help me plow through sources and hoped one of us would find significant information.

Camille joined us. She was already wearing her coat and gloves. "Everyone's coming to our house for breakfast tomorrow before leaving," she said.

And just like that, Christmas day was as good as over. If only it would have lasted longer. Weren't there supposed to be twelve days of Christmas?

"Julia and I will be there, but Crane will be on duty," I said.

Camille sighed. "We'll miss him, but somebody has to keep the Corners safe."

She was thinking of speeders and criminals. Unfortunately, Crane couldn't capture and confine ghosts, but maybe they had made their yearly appearance in Foxglove Corners and moved on. So far, nothing untoward had happened. It must be true that spirits kept their distance from mortals on these holy days.

"We're going to welcome the new year in at the Hunt Club Inn," Brent said. "I reserved a room."

"Who's we?"

"Whoever wants to come."

"That'll be something to look forward to," Lucy said.

"Good food, good wine—no champagne—confetti, and noisemakers," he added.

It sounded good, but if Crane was on duty, I planned to stay home and wait for his shift to be over. We'd celebrate together, and I said a silent prayer that the last holiday of the old year would be ghost-free.

Brent spied Annica across the room and left us to speak to her. Like a shadow, Nova moved with him. Already she adored him. Could she sense that his ownership of her had been challenged?

I told Lucy what he had revealed about the man whose wife had surrendered Nova to a shelter.

"I wouldn't believe him," Lucy said. "Something else is going on." She turned to the painting. "There's a collie in the picture. She looks like Nova, white blaze and all."

"I saw a dog the first time the sleigh appeared on Windemere Road, but not after that."

"So there was a dog when the four young people set out on their doomed ride. I wonder what happened to her?"

"I hope I can find out," I said. "What we have is a mystery within our mystery."

~ * ~

Crane's family set out for home the same way they'd arrived, in two vehicles. The men were already in their cars, letting them warm up. Because it had started snowing again, Aunt Betsy and Suanna said their goodbyes in the vestibule of the yellow Victorian.

"I'm kind of sorry I didn't get to see the sleigh," Suanna said.

So much for her not believing in ghosts.

"This has been one of the best Christmases ever," she added. "I love your little town."

"Come back anytime," I said. "There's always something happening in Foxglove Corners."

"I'd love to do that."

"You, too, Aunt Becky."

"I will, but you and Crane should spend next Christmas in Tennessee with us."

"We'd have to find a good live-in dog sitter," I said. "We can't impose on Camille that long."

"Maybe you can work something out."

I had a vision, a ludicrous one, of buying a bus and making the long drive south with our eight collies. No, that would never work.

"It's a long time until next Christmas," I said. "A whole year."

Hugs and final goodbyes, and Aunt Becky and Suanna tramped through the snow to the waiting cars.

I closed the door before the wind could blow snow inside. "I'm going to miss them. I wish they lived nearer. Say in Ohio."

Camille had donned her 'Come woo me' apron and disappeared into the kitchen.

"Let's give Camille a hand with the dishes," I said. "Then would you like to go to the library with me? It shouldn't be crowded."

"Are we on the trail of the phantom sleigh?"

"Of course. Also, the artist. I'm wondering if he was a contemporary of the sleigh riders. Who knows? He might have been staying at the Faraday house."

"I'm game," she said. "Just let me grab a notebook."

Camille reappeared with a large box. "Between us we made way too many cookies, Jennet. I sent some along in a lunch for our travelers, set some aside for you and Crane, and I'm still drowning in them."

I took the box. It was heavier than it looked. "I'll split them with Miss Eidt," I said. "We're off to the library."

"I think I know why. Let me issue a warning: *Let sleeping dogs lie.*"

"What are you saying?" Julia asked.

"Simply that all this interest and action on your part may stir up something better left alone."

"You sound like Lucy," I said. "But this is one mystery I can't leave alone. And if it wants to get me, it will."

Twenty-four

'Twas the day after Christmas and a deep holiday silence hung over the Corners. The library's parking lot was almost empty, an unplowed expanse of white. The few cars and a trail of jumbled boot prints leading up to the porch were the only indications that the old white Victorian was open for business.

Julia pulled on her gloves and opened the door while I reached for the box of cookies. "It looks like we'll have peace and quiet for our research."

"Good," I said. "No distractions."

Snowflakes fell in a lazy trek to the ground as we made our way up to the porch. It was a good day to spend with books, even if that entailed conducting a dubious search for an obscure artist.

Blackberry, the cat, had left her customary place on the porch to crouch behind a bush. You couldn't miss her, a motionless splash of jet black in a world of white.

"Poor kitty," Julia said. "She'll freeze out here."

I had no such fear. "Blackberry was a feral cat before Miss Eidt adopted her. She'll be all right."

"Here, kitty, kitty..." Julia called.

But Blackberry sped away, disappearing around the side of the library.

"She's still half-wild," I said.

I pushed open the heavy door, and the warmth and coziness drew us in. Miss Eidt sat at her desk drinking from a large mug decorated with holly berries. She looked unusually bright in a silky red dress. Her necklace must be new, a long rope of antique gold, pearls, and red stones.

The library looked bright, too, all the decorations still crisp and fresh.

The easy chairs were occupied by faithful patrons catching up on the day's news or settling in for a long morning's read.

"Merry Christmas, girls," Miss Eidt said. "Did you have a nice holiday?"

"The best ever." I gave her the box of cookies. "We brought you some homemade treats from Camille's kitchen and mine."

She removed the lid eagerly. "Oh, my!"

"Camille made the fancy ones," I said. "The angel wings and those little rolls filled with nuts and something delicious. I don't know what it is."

"Mince meat," Julia supplied.

"I'm still researching the phantom sleigh," I said. "We're hoping to find something I missed."

"That reminds me...I found an old article that should interest you. Someone cut off the ending, though."

"I didn't know anyone else used your vertical file."

"Apparently somebody did. I don't know when it happened. I don't even remember filing it. Maybe Darla did. She worked for me before Debbie. Now...where is it?"

She rummaged through the papers in her desk drawer, finally withdrawing a brittle clipping on yellowing paper.

"Handle it with care," Miss Eidt said.

I set the article on the desk where a ray of light fought its way through the red leaves of an enormous poinsettia plant.

The date was handwritten in black ink: January 24, 1938.

CLUE EMERGES IN CHRISTMAS DISAPPEARANCE

A sighting by Mister Byron Holloway of Foxglove Corners may shed light on the month-long disappearance of four people who failed to return from a Christmas Eve sleigh ride last month. Mister Holloway saw the missing sleigh and its occupants on Frost Lake Road late yesterday afternoon.

"I was outside shoveling snow when I heard sleigh bells and music," Mister Holloway said. "Then I saw the sleigh. The riders were singing a Christmas song. I thought about the missing people right away. Were they just joyriding across the countryside for a month while their family mourned them for dead?"

In a related story...

"Drat," I said. "The rest of it is gone. What kind of related story? And what happened to the sleigh? Did it move on or disappear or what?"

"What do you make of it, Jennet?" Miss Eidt asked.

"That this could be the first recorded appearance of the phantom sleigh. January twenty-fourth,1938."

"Yes," Julia said. "They wouldn't just keep riding around for a month. What would they do for food?"

"And I assumed the police were on the lookout for them."

"This intrigues me," Miss Eidt said. "I'm going to make a new folder for the haunted sleigh mystery, and I'll help you look for more material."

That was good news. One of us was bound to find something, if it existed.

"I bought an oil painting that I'm sure was inspired by the ride," I said. "I'd like to find some background information on the artist. He signed his work G. Allemand."

"I've never heard of him," she said "but we have a new book on Michigan artists. You could check that out."

Around us, the conversational hum rose a few decibels. Four teenaged girls had entered the library and commandeered one of the library's largest table. They were busy divesting themselves of winter outerwear, letting their coats drip melting snow on the floor.

Of course. Schools were on vacation.

One of them cried, "Oh, look at the doll house!"

They rose to admire it. "Such teeny, tiny ornaments!"

Miss Eidt sprang to indignant life before the speaker could move the mini candy cane. "Look but *do not* touch, girls." She turned to me. "I guess I'm going to have to post a sign. You go ahead. You know where everything is, Jennet."

I did, but this time I looked for file folders I hadn't searched before. 'Cold Cases,' 'Transportation in the Early Twentieth Century,' 'Oddities' and even 'Dogs.'

Miss Eidt came in to bring the box of cookies and boil water for tea, then left us when we heard the clamor of books falling to the floor.

An hour later, the file folders had been emptied and their contents scrutinized. I'd learned several fascinating facts but none that would shed enlightenment on the mystery I pursued. If the phantom sleigh had materialized at any time after the one-month anniversary of its disappearance, no one had informed the papers.

"It doesn't seem likely that it waited almost a hundred years to appear again," Julia said.

I thought about that. With the long stretches of woods and unpopulated areas in Foxglove Corners, the sleigh could easily have passed by unnoticed several times, its bells and the riders' songs gone unheard.

Another thought came to me. "Time on another plane may be different. Maybe to the riders, it's only been a year."

"That's weird," Julia said with a shiver.

"I'm just guessing."

The artist G. Allemand remained a mystery. Obviously, he was a minor painter, perhaps an amateur. Anyone could create a stunning scene and not earn even a short mention in the history books.

I began to gather the files in a neat stack. "We've done all we can for today. We need a new angle."

"I'm getting hungry," Julia said. "Let's grab a sandwich at Clovers. Or do you need to go home?"

I glanced at my watch. "A quick lunch sounds good. Let me check out the book on Michigan artists first."

While I headed for the Fine Arts section, Julia waited, admiring the doll house. I found the book, a fresh, shiny volume, and checked it out, then headed for the door when a familiar voice made me wish my timing had been better.

"I hear you have a new mystery, Jennet," Edwina Endicott said. "Care to talk about it?"

Twenty-five

Edwina always reminded me of a wraith with her fondness for colorless, trailing dresses. Today, her black coat was unbuttoned to reveal a gray sweater and a wispy white scarf expertly tied around her neck. A silvery gray midi-skirt dropped down to her ankles.

"Edwina," I said. "What are you talking about? There's no mystery."

"That's not what I heard."

Her tone challenged me to contradict her. I had no intention of telling anyone but my closest friends about my phantom sleigh. Certainly not Edwina.

"Where did you hear that?" I asked.

She shrugged. "Oh, around. I don't remember exactly."

Because she wasn't telling the truth? Fishing for information was more likely, hoping I'd fall into the neat little trap she'd set for me.

From her desk, Miss Eidt gave us the quiet-in-the library look she reserved for chatty schoolgirls.

"Let's move on," I said and headed for the vestibule where we could talk without disturbing anyone. I hoped to convince Edwina that I wasn't attempting to solve a mystery.

"I've been busy entertaining family from out of town," I said.

"If you say so."

She didn't believe me. Was it possible that one of my friends had let something slip?

Julia met us in the vestibule. "You're not leaving me behind, I hope."

"No, of course not," I said, knowing that I had to make the introductions and prolong the encounter.

"This is my sister, Edwina. Julia, I'd like you to meet Edwina Endicott."

"That's Edwina Endicott, Ghost Hunter," she said. "Let me give you one of my cards."

Well, this was new. She drew two cards out of her purse. "Here's one for you, Jennet. I just had them printed."

Julia scanned the card, doing her best to hold back a smile. "You're really a ghost hunter?"

"I am."

"How's business?" she asked.

"Slow," Edwina said. "People in the spirit world make themselves scarce during the holidays. They don't like all the commotion and noise."

"What do you do with a ghost when you catch one?"

I glanced at Julia, hoping my look would convince her to curb her curiosity. She ignored me.

"I don't actually catch a spirit," Edwina said. "What I do is try to find evidence of paranormal activity. Say someone is being haunted. They contact me. If I can find out why the ghost is restless, I can put a stop to its antics. Hopefully."

In spite of myself, I was fascinated. "How do you do that? Surely not with an exorcism."

"No, casting out devils is not in my job description," she said. "Once I determine why the spirit can't cross over to the world beyond, I give them the help they need. It varies with the individual."

This didn't tell me anything. I wanted to ask why again but decided not to. Her explanation would only be convoluted.

Julia said, "That's amazing." She sounded sincere. For all I knew, she *was* sincere. My sister was, above all, kind. But I hadn't meant to engage Edwina in a discussion of her avocation.

"Nice meeting you, Edwina." Julia opened the door, and the wreath with its vintage wood figures clanked against wood. "We should be on our way, Jennet."

"Yes, we have a lunch engagement. Have a Happy New Year, Edwina," I added.

She didn't follow us out to the parking lot but waited inside. Maybe she wasn't ready to leave the library yet, and had hoped to extend our conversation. At any rate, we were outside now. Edwina must live in the library when she wasn't helping spirits find their peace. I always seemed to run into her, usually in the Supernatural section or the Gothic Nook.

"It's snowing harder," Julia said, then lowered her voice even though Edwina couldn't possibly hear us. "What a strange woman. She's serious about that ghost catching business, isn't she?"

"I think so, and I also believe she has some connection with the spirit world. She saw Violet Randall, the girl who lived in the pink Victorian that burned to the ground."

Violet haunted Huron Court with her collie. Julia knew the story. In fact, she had participated in it.

"Edwina thinks I have a new mystery," I said. "She claims she heard it but wouldn't say where."

"I don't see how she could have."

"We were talking about a phantom sleigh the last time we met. Maybe she's guessing."

As we made our way through falling snow to the car, I gave some thought to an idea that had been bouncing around in my head. Edwina had annoyed me in the past, but with her knowledge of otherworldly matters and ability to see spirits, which I didn't doubt, she might be able to help me solved the mystery of the sleigh. In some as-yet-undetermined way.

"I could eat a whole dinner," Julia said as we reached the car. "I'll clear the window while you warm up the car."

I was happy to take care of the heating while Julia sent the snow flying back into the air. While waiting for warmth and visibility, I came to a decision. If it became necessary, I would call Edwina and see if she could catch up with the four ghosts who rode in the sleigh.

~ * ~

The little restaurant on Crispian Road sat in a surround of snow, its green clover border bright amid all the white. There weren't many cars in the lot, so we could probably be in and out in record time.

We entered to the ringing of the clover chimes and found Annica filling the dessert carousel, which was her favorite job. The offerings were on the skimpy side as Clovers had been closed on Christmas. Still, the generous slices of cake glistened with holly berries on red and green frosting.

Annica wore a pair of earrings I hadn't seen before, little Christmas wreaths with tiny multi-colored stones. She tapped one with her finger. "Do you like my new earrings? Brent gave them to me for Christmas."

Then the stones must be real—emeralds, rubies sapphires, and diamonds. Brent didn't buy costume jewelry.

"He has good taste," I said, thinking how pretty Annica looked with her red-gold hair against the brilliant gemstones.

When we were settled in my favorite booth that looked out on the snowy woods across the road, Julia glanced at the overhead menu. "We'll have sandwiches. What's good?"

"The turkey club, without a doubt."

"That's what I'll have then with hot tea. Julia?"

"The same."

Annica jotted down our order. "I don't have classes until after New Year's day. Maybe I can help you with the sleigh."

"I'm at a standstill," I said. "I was hoping to find background information on the artist who painted the oil painting I gave Lucy. At this point, I guess all I can do is wait and see if the phantom sleigh materializes again."

"You bought the painting at the Green House of Antiques, didn't you?" Annica asked.

"Yes on Christmas Eve. Why?"

"They're having a major sale of holiday merchandise. All green-starred items are half off. I'm going to stop in there after work."

"They almost never have sales," I said. "We should go, Julia."

Mentally, I apologized to my waiting collies. Camille would let them out, but we'd already been gone all morning.

"I'd like that," Julia said. "They had some gorgeous vintages dresses. I want to wear something special to Brent's New Year's Eve gathering."

Julia would look spectacular in a vintage dress. I already had something special. My red dress with my new jewelry would do very well. If I went to the Hunt Club Inn, that is. It depended on Crane's schedule.

"And maybe one of the clerks knows who G. Allemand was," I said.

Twenty-six

The window of the Green House of Antiques was an ever-changing delight to look at. The owner had added an oversized red pillowcase from which an eclectic mixture spilled out onto the imitation snow: a variety of old-time brooches, storybook dolls, a fancy evening purse, a kaleidoscope, and a miniature rocking horse.

The books that had formed a pathway to Santa's throne lay jumbled together in a high mound at the window's edge. All at sale prices.

The bells on the door announced our arrival, but no one paid attention to two more customers. About thirty sales seekers moved through the shop scooping up bargains with only three clerks to wait on them. I didn't imagine anyone would have time to answer a question about an obscure artist, but if I appeared to be a paying customer with a book in my hand, someone would be bound to notice me.

I began to seek out books with dull, tattered, or smudged covers which marked them as vintage. Scattered throughout the shop were copies of *Maida's Little House*, *Emily Climbs*, *Emily's Quest*, Penny Parker mysteries, and the Outdoor Girls.

Moving to a table laden with a little bit of everything, I flipped through a stack of framed oil paintings and watercolors. To my amazement, among them I found my sleigh scene! Rather another sleigh scene similar to the one I'd given to Lucy. I lifted it up to the light so I could see it clearly.

It was the same sleigh with the same four riders in the same locale or one very similar—with a collie running alongside it. Only the sleigh and the people were slightly larger, their features sharper, and the expressions seemed different. Apprehensive? Perhaps fearful?

I studied the canvas carefully. It was as if the occupants knew something was about to go terribly wrong with their merry holiday sleigh ride. But surely I was imposing my own skewered interpretation on the artist's details, knowing what I did about the disappearance.

This painting, too, was the work of the elusive G. Allemand. The green star attached to the frame indicated that its price was fifty percent off the original.

I had no intentions of buying it, but now more than ever I wanted to know its history.

Why had the artist painted the scene twice? Because he so obsessed by the story of the sleigh? Perhaps he had painted others, variations of the theme. I searched the remaining canvases, all of which were snowscapes or fanciful depictions of Santa, toys, Christmas trees, and angels, but this was the only one by G. Allemand.

I looked for Julia in the crowd and saw her at a rack of period dresses. Weaving my way through the shoppers, I said, "You won't believe it. I just saw another sleigh painting."

"I thought it was one of a kind."

"No one said so. Actually, there wasn't anyone to say anything. "

"What do think this means?" she asked.

"Maybe an artist is like an author who writes books in a series. He can't stop with one. Or this was a subject close to his heart, a mystery he wanted to solve but obviously didn't."

"On the other hand, sleighs are common enough for Christmas pictures," Julia pointed out.

"Come see the painting," I said.

"In a minute. What do you think of this dress for New Year's Eve?"

The one she'd selected was pure vintage, pale florals on an ivory background with a low scoop neck, a lace bodice, and three-quarter length sleeves.

"It's perfect," I said. "You'll look like Glinda, the Good Witch of the East. Or a bride."

"And I found a brooch to go with it."

"You're all set, then."

She took the dress from the rack and held it up off the floor. "I saw it when we were here on Christmas Eve. At this price, I can't pass it up."

Back at the table, Julia and I examined the oil painting. After a while, to me at least, it seemed almost to move, a drift of snow slipping down to the ground at the breath of an invisible wind. I could imagine the brush of snow on my outstretched hand.

"It's exactly like the one you gave to Lucy," Julia said.

"Don't you think the expressions on the riders' faces are different in this scene?" I asked.

"In what way?"

"Like they know what's going to happen around the next bend in the road."

"I'd have to see the two paintings together," she said.

"We can't do that unless I buy it, and that isn't going to happen. But I can pretend I'm interested. That won't be a lie. I am."

"They don't look very happy," Julia said.

Clutching a hastily chosen Beverly Gray book and the painting, lest another eager buyer lay claim to it, I waited until a clerk whose nametag identified her as Ellalyn finished advising her customer on the benefit of owning an old, outdated globe.

The customer thanked her but didn't appear convinced. "Let me think about it," she said and made her escape.

"I'd like this book," I said, "and I have a question about this painting."

Ellalyn had a long blonde ponytail and the bright-eyed eagerness of a young girl at her first job. She wore one of the sale brooches on her black sweater.

"That is a treasure," she said. "We had two and sold one earlier this morning."

Which meant there were three in existence that I knew of.

"Can you tell me anything about the artist?" I asked.

"Not too much," Ellalyn said. "She's kind of a recluse, but she gave us a load of stuff to sell on commission last month."

"She?" I repeated. "The artist is a woman? She's still living?"

"She was, around Thanksgiving. Her name is Grace Allemand. She lives in Foxglove Corners. I don't know if she'd be willing to talk to you, but you can always call and ask her."

Finally. A bona fide clue. It had been a long time coming, but Grace Allemand might lead me to the story behind the ill-fated ride. At least I could hope.

"I'll do that," I said, "and thank you."

"Do you want the painting, then?" she asked.

"Mm, no. Just the book."

~ * ~

Grace Allemand lived in the Frost Lake Estates, the relatively new development to which Alethea Venn had recently moved. It was too much to expect that I'd dial her number and make immediate contact with her. She was out of town, her voice mail announced, and promised to return all calls as soon as possible.

I wasn't discouraged. Far from it. After all, good things come to those who wait. I slipped my phone back in my purse.

"Are you going to tell her that you saw the phantom sleigh?" Julia asked as she hung her new dress in the guest room closet.

"Eventually. I'll tell her how much I love her sleigh painting and ask what inspired it."

"But you don't love it. You gave it away."

"She doesn't have to know that, and if it hadn't made Crane uncomfortable, I'd have kept it."

"You know best," Julia said. "I guess."

"If I lead with a ghost sighting, she'll think I'm crazy."

"You can ask her why she made three copies of the same scene."

"Yes, and why she's selling them now. And if there are any more."

"She'll wonder why you're interrogating her," Julia warned.

"I'll have to be subtle."

"You'll manage." She closed the closet door. "What'll we make for dinner?"

"I defrosted a roast, and we have potatoes and carrots."

Cooking dinner ceased to be a chore when I had someone to help me. We had dessert covered, having baked pies and more cookies yesterday.

With dinner preparations underway, Julia took Halley, Sky and Star for a walk, taking advantage of a brief lull in the snow, while I neatened the house. Before long, the day caught up with me. I sat in the rocker admiring the decorations and the way the blue light shone on the sleigh ornament from my secret Santa.

My eyelids felt heavy. I didn't want to fall asleep. But I didn't want to get up either.

Except I was cold. So cold. How could one be so cold and still be alive?

Through my dream, sleigh bells rang, cutting into the air with sharp, clear notes.

No! Not again!

It was snowing. I sat between Margaret and Edmond in the sleigh, shivering in my warm wool dress. Where was my coat? My gloves and scarf?

The horses pranced down a snowy lane at a good pace. We were approaching a curve in the road.

"Shouldn't we turn back, Nicholas?" Auralee asked.

He turned back to look at her. "You're not afraid of a little snow, are you?"

"I'm not afraid, only getting cold. I want to be home before the snow gets worse."

I don't belong here, I thought.

"Take us back, please," Margaret said.

I don't belong here, I said aloud and tried to rise but to my horror discovered I couldn't move. And I didn't hear my voice.

Edmund pulled me closer to him. "Sit still, Auralee, you'll fall out."

He was talking to me, looking at me. How could he think I was Auralee?

Dear Lord, I couldn't move. Couldn't talk.

Nicholas began singing:

Over the river and through the woods

To Grandfather's house we go...

Shouldn't it be Grandmother's house?

We were almost at the point in the lane where the curve began. Was this where it had happened? Whatever happened to catapult the sleigh into the Twilight Zone?

Twenty-seven

A wet paw lay heavily on my lap. I opened my eyes, annoyed that I had fallen asleep in the middle of the day. And that dream. That horrible dream. I'd better forget it. My hands felt as if they were encased in ice.

Julia was back from her walk, and the collies who had accompanied her were shaking themselves vigorously. Snow flew in every direction. Apparently it had started snowing again, forcing them to cut the walk short.

"The snow is going to go on falling forever," she lamented.

"Well, it's winter."

A safe answer. Every day it snowed a little, adding a fresh white layer to the landscape. At least no blizzards lurked in the forecast.

"I don't really mind it," she said. "A walk in the snow is fun as long as you have a nice warm house to come home to. How's the roast doing?"

I lifted the top of the roasting pan. "Almost done. Would you like some hot chocolate?"

"With marshmallows? A resounding yes."

Julia began singing, *It's a marshmallow world in the winter* while I reached for the cocoa tin.

The dogs were barking at the front door.

"What now?" But I suspected I knew the identity of our guest. The irresistible aroma of the pot roast had a long reach.

Julia peered out the living room window. "It's Brent's old car," Julia called.

"Don't let him hear you describe it that way. It's his prized vintage Plymouth Belvedere."

"He has his collie with him," she said.

I added another half cup of cocoa powder while Julia opened the door.

"Hello, all! Happy day after Christmas!" he boomed out. "I came for dinner."

"Come on in then."

He set a bag from Pluto's Gourmet Pet Shop on the kitchen table and sank into an oak chair, freeing Nova from her leash, whereupon she began a 'Chase me' game with Velvet. The other dogs lay around the table close to the treats, waiting for them to be dispensed.

"What's on the menu today?" he asked.

"A surprise."

"I need some cheering up on a gloomy day."

Gloomy? The snow had stopped again, and a weak sun peeked out from behind the clouds. This was curious as Brent never let the weather affect him. Something else troubled him then.

"What's wrong?" I asked.

"That guy who wants Nova back paid me another visit at the barn this morning."

"But I see you still have her."

"I take her with me all the time. See what you think, Jennet. His little boy is sick. He may not make it. He's been grieving for his dog. They told him she ran away from home."

"Nice parents. Didn't you say his wife dumped Nova at a shelter?"

"That's what he said. Now it seems she had a change of heart."

I gave the hot cocoa a stir. "This whole story is suspicious. Also, when you leave a dog at a shelter, you give up your right to her, as far as I'm concerned. Did he say why his wife surrendered Nova?"

Brent shrugged. "She didn't want a female. Didn't want any kind of dog."

"And now she does?" I shook my head. "Like I said, suspicious."

I believed the man wanted Nova back but didn't believe his reason.

"If the little boy dies without being reunited with Nova I think I'll regret it all my life," Brent said. "What should I do?"

"Don't do anything until you know more. Find out the real story. For all you know, this man may not even have a sick child or a wife, for that matter. By the way, we can't keep calling him this man. What's his name?"

"Clifton. Red Clifton. I can't figure out why he wants Nova. She's a real sweetheart, but she's no puppy. She isn't show quality. Nova looks like dozens of other collies. Besides, she's mine," he added in a voice that was, for Brent, soft.

"Promise me you won't give her up," I said.

"I don't want to, but the kid..."

"First, make sure there *is* a kid. If he exists, find out about this critical illness. Did it just come on?"

"He said something about cancer. He wasn't specific about the details."

"He doesn't have to be. That one word says it all. You should also ask questions about the wife."

"I told him I'd have to think about it. That he couldn't just uproot a dog who'd already gotten accustomed to her new home."

"What did he say to that?"

"He said I had plenty of other collies. I didn't need one more, and he did. For his son. He said it didn't matter what the dog felt."

Velvet and Nova ran into the kitchen, circled the table three times, and took off into the dining room."

"Careful around the tree." I braced myself for the clink of fragile ornaments breaking, but it didn't happen. The two friends made another rowdy entrance into the kitchen.

I turned the burner on low under the saucepan. "Have some hot chocolate with us," I said. "Chocolate makes everything better."

"I think I will, but I feel better already."

I knew what would make him feel better still. Julia and I had baked cookies last night, New Year's bells in three sizes sprinkled with red and green sugar. I emptied the contents of one of the cookie tins and stacked them onto a plate.

"I still think of Nova as the dog who ran with the sleigh," I said, "even though I know she can't be."

I remembered, too, that in one painting a collie who resembled Nova *did* appear to be running alongside the phantom sleigh, and that the first time I'd seen the sleigh on Windemere Road, I'd also seen the collie. Both apparitions.

Don't complicate an already complicated situation, I told myself.

~ * ~

We had a good dinner and a pleasant evening with Brent and Julia. Brent went home, somewhat optimistic about his future with Nova, Julia went to bed, and the snow started falling again.

Crane rounded up the dogs to take them outside while I traveled through the first floor, turning out lights. The night was no different from any other, and I looked forward to a long, dreamless sleep.

Cold air and snow woke me. Snow falling on my hair, landing on my bare hands, covering my wedding ring.

Where were my gloves. I was...Oh, no. Back in the sleigh. Edmund's arm lay heavily on my shoulder. He'd just called me Auralee.

I already had this dream. I didn't want to be here again in this wind-whipped white world. Could I possibly jump down from the sleigh? First, I would have to be able to move. Could I move?

I would land in one of those handy snowdrifts, and then...

Edmund shouted over the howling wind. "Nicholas! I don't remember all these fir trees. Are we going home a different way?"

Nicholas shouted something back. I couldn't hear him.

Edmund said, "We're not lost, are we?"

Nicholas' reply, caught by the wind, went whirling away.

At my side, Margaret asked, "Are we close to the hall?"

A gust of icy wind blew a wave of snow over the sleigh. I couldn't see. How could Nicholas guide the horses through this malestrom?

The horse knows the way

To carry the sleigh

O'er white and drifted snow...

"Come on, everyone," Edmond said. "Let's sing. You know the song."

The sleigh made a sharp turn, following the curve. The bells screamed. Abruptly, the snow squall subsided. The heaviness on my shoulder lightened. Turned sharp. Unpleasant.

I wiped snow from my face with my bare hand and saw that my companions had turned to skeletons. The hand on my shoulder now consisted of bones.

Twenty-eight

I awoke, knowing I'd been dreaming but still feeling as if I had jumped out of a moving sleigh and landed on the hard, frozen ground. I was cold. In my sleep, I'd pushed the covers to one side, but it was the residual cold of the dream that pursued me into a waking state.

I pulled the flannel sheet and blanket up to my shoulders and forced myself to breathe deeply and relax. To let the ghastly images fade. I had just had the second part of a terrifying dream. This was strange. How many dreams have sequels? Stranger still would be a theoretical third part.

I didn't believe for one second that the answer to my questions had been revealed to me in a dream. It was simply that I'd become obsessed with the phantom sleigh and its depiction in Grace Allemand's art. They seemed to occupy my every thought.

However, suppose that my dream was trying to tell me what had happened to the doomed sleigh?

I lay back and reconstructed the story. The sleigh riders had encountered a snowstorm. Auralee and Margaret were frightened. Edmund tried to keep their spirits up by singing a holiday song. Nicholas found himself guiding the horses down an unfamiliar country lane. His last utterance, which I hadn't been able to hear, was probably a confession that they were lost.

Thankfully, the dream ended before I experienced whatever lay beyond the curve in the road. I wanted to know what happened but not to be a part of it.

I needed to consult with Lucy. Soon. But at the moment, all I could do was go back to sleep. And not dream.

How wonderful it would be if we could order our night's dreams the way we ordered pizza. If that were possible, I would dream about…

The phone's melodious notes alerted me to the time. I had fallen into a deep, dreamless sleep that left me refreshed. The day lay before me, one of the last days of the old year. I resolved to make it significant.

Still, the last part of the dream held me in an unrelenting grip. My companions turned to skeletons. What did that portend for me?

~ * ~

I hoped Grace Allemand would return my call but wasn't counting on it. I was, therefore, surprised to hear an unfamiliar voice on the phone the next morning.

"Am I speaking to Mrs. Jennet Ferguson? Good. I just listened to your message. I'm so pleased that you're happy with *Dark Sleigh Ride*. Thank you so much for taking the time to tell me."

That sounded like a gracious, but formal, thank you for an unexpected compliment. I needed to keep the conversation going.

"I find your work intriguing as well as beautiful," I said, "especially since I discovered two almost identical paintings."

"Yes, I've painted the same ride at different times. Each one is slightly different."

"Were you aware of the four young people who disappeared in 1938?" I asked.

A pause. "I am. In fact, that's my great family mystery."

I searched for the right way to present my proposition. "I'd like to write an article about the background of your painting."

That was true. At present, I was working on a book about the supernatural phenomena I'd encountered since moving to Foxglove

Corners. It was almost finished, and naturally the phantom sleigh would be included.

An alert note entered her tone. "Are you a reporter?"

"No, I'm a high school English teacher."

"I can see why you're attracted to the sleigh story," she said. "It's a chilling Christmas mystery."

"Do you suppose we could meet for lunch?"

Her answer came after another brief pause. "Oh, I'm afraid I don't go out much these days. I don't like to drive in the winter."

But she'd just been out of town...

"What if you didn't have to drive? I could pick you up. We could go a little restaurant I'm fond of."

Before I could expound on the virtues of Clovers, she said, "Or you could come to my house. I love to have company."

That would be better than meeting at Clovers. We would have privacy. Comfortable in her own home, Mrs. Allemand might be inspired to reveal more of her story than she would in a crowded restaurant.

"I'd like that," I said. "What time were you thinking of?"

"How does tomorrow sound? Around noon?"

"Perfect," I said.

It was about time things started going my way.

~ * ~

The next morning, I turned on Estate Drive and drove a half mile before seeing the first house in the Frost Lake development. Built in Queen Anne style, it sat on a hilltop far from the road. Mature blue spruces and carefully spaced hardwoods were strung with Christmas lights, obviously not turned on during the day.

The road, plowed but uneven, curved gracefully through land that alternated between neatly landscaped houses and stretches of brooding woods.

I wondered which of the estates belonged to Brent's friend, Alethea Venn, but not for long. The address Mrs. Allemand had given me loomed ahead. The house was a handsome English Tudor that looked incongruous in the snowswept Michigan setting.

The woman who came to the door was small, silver-haired and dressed in black.

"Good morning," she said. "I'm Lily. Mrs. Allemand is in the sitting room."

How formal. A maid or housekeeper to answer the door...but the elegant Tudor mansion called for one.

Grace Allemand sat in a cozy rocker, a little like my own, with a cane leaning on a nearby table. The table also held a small decorated Christmas tree to mark the season and a creche with multiple figures. And on the wall above a fireplace...

I stifled a gasp as I saw a much larger oil painting of the sleigh with its four riders. In this ornately framed version, the faces were truly vivid as were the expressions on them. Grace had captured her subjects at a fearful moment.

I studied the painting silently, focusing on the faces. Auralee's eyes were bright with tears. Edmund held Margaret's hand, and Nicholas was even more incredibly handsome.

Grace noticed my absorption in her work. "You're looking at the last and best of the Dark Sleigh Ride paintings," she said.

"It's magnificent."

The painting dominated the room and this wall, as it appeared to dominate her life.

"Was the sleigh ever found?" I asked, even though I knew the answer.

"Never, in all the years. Not even a piece of it. They were all lost. My cousins, their young men. Even the horses and Nana."

"Nana being?"

"Auralee's collie."

The dog who ran with the sleigh.

"Can you tell me anything about that time and your family members?" I asked.

"We were all happy and excited about Christmas. There was to be a party at Faraday Hall. Nicholas was home from college. He was studying medicine. Edmond was a neighbor of the Faradays, and Margaret had traveled up from Louisiana for the winter.

"I was too young to be considered one of their group, but I remember them so clearly. My aunts were both so pretty and full of life. And Nicholas...I had a crush on him. It was his idea to take the sleigh out that day. Beyond that, all I know is that it never returned. The time after was all a muddle."

"Are you aware that Foxglove Corners is a place where strange things happen? I asked.

"Like our sleigh?"

"Ghost stories in general. Disappearances on Brandymere Road, for instance. It's said that travelers reach a point where the road melts away and they drop off the end of the earth."

"I know about Brandymere, and I'd think it was all nonsense, but considering what happened to my family members, I'm a believer."

This was my cue. "I'm especially interested in the story because about a month ago I saw the sleigh and the four riders."

She stared at me in wonder, incredulous. Then practicality took over. "How can you be sure it wasn't some other sleigh? One of the farmers rents out his old-time sleigh for rides this time of the year."

"I'm sure," I said. "Everything looked exactly like you portray it in your painting, and it just sort of melted away."

I held back the fact that the first time I'd seen the sleigh, it had forced me off the road and into danger. That was, I have to admit, mostly my fault.

"I'd give anything if I could see them again," Grace said. "Even their spirits."

Suddenly she seemed dejected, almost on the point of tears.

I quickly headed in another direction, "Your painting is so lifelike. It's a real masterpiece. I can practically feel the cold and the snow. It seems like the people could step out of the canvas and talk to me."

"To reveal what happened to them and where they are now. Wouldn't that be wonderful?"

"You might have been working from live models," I added.

"It was done from memory and pictures. Edmund was an amateur photographer. His photos aren't the best quality, but when added to my memories I was able to paint a good likeness of them."

"It appears that the sleigh is still traveling through Foxglove Corners," I said. Maybe I'll see them again. Nicholas, Auralee..."

The horses, I thought. *The collie, Nana.*

"Then why can't I see them?" Grace wanted to know.

"There haven't been any documented sightings that I know of. Oh, except for one in an old news story."

"It's holiday time again," Grace said. "We just passed the anniversary of their disappearance. If you see them again, you will tell me, won't you?"

"I'll be certain to."

"I remember that day like it was yesterday. I recall what Auralee said to me just before they left. She said, 'You can come with us the next time, Gracie'."

"I'm still waiting," Grace said.

Twenty-nine

I had forgotten that in my initial conversation with Grace I'd mentioned our getting together for lunch. Apparently, she remembered. At this precise moment, Lily, the maid or companion—or whichever she was—wheeled in a cart covered with a silver coffee service and a platter of sandwiches. A dozen Christmas-decorated petit fours graced a plate in a pretty snowflake pattern.

"Thank you, Lily," Grace said. "I hope you like turkey and ham salad, Jennet. They're my favorites. Lily bakes the bread and dessert."

All of a sudden, I remembered I was hungry. "It all looks wonderful."

Lily stayed to pour coffee and offer cream and sugar, both of which I declined.

As we ate, I mulled over what Grace had said. 'You can come with us the next time.' If someone had said that to me and later vanished into the unknown, I'd be concerned about an ominous inner meaning. But Grace recalled only the poignancy of her outing with the grown-ups that had never materialized.

For some reason, my mind drifted back to one of my earliest sleigh dreams, when I'd been staring at my Secret Santa sleigh ornament and imagined a voice saying, 'Come join us.' Then I recalled my most recent dream, sitting in the sleigh beside Edmund, feeling the sharpness of his skeletal arm on my shoulder.

Could the doomed sleigh riders be hoping others would join them? Were they capable of making that happen?

No. Impossible. Unless they were demons.

I let the grisly thought drift away and glanced at the painting above the mantel. It should have made the living room cozy but instead, it communicated only a reminder of the mystery, of the frosty day, and the snowstorm. The cold of loss everlasting.

Grace was looking at me, waiting for a response to a question I hadn't heard.

"Sorry," I said. "Would you please repeat that? I got lost in your painting for a moment."

"I only wondered how all they looked in your vision. Besides lifelike."

"The first time I saw the sleigh, they appeared to be happy. The way you'd be if you were embarking on a joyride in the snow with your friends. They were singing a Christmas song. Later...Well..."

I paused in my tale, needing to separate my dream from the actual sighting. I certainly didn't want to tell Grace that my companions had turned to skeletons. "Later, not so much."

Grace helped herself to one of the petit fours and passed the plate to me. "In those days, we didn't have advance warnings of severe weather. If Nicholas had known about a snowstorm on the way, he wouldn't have suggested the sleigh ride. Life would have been different. Auralee might have married Nicholas. Anyone could see she was sweet on him.

"Edmund might have persuaded Margaret to stay in Foxglove Corners or he'd have gone back down South with her. Sometimes, I think of the families they might have had. But forgive me. I don't mean to be maudlin."

"Can you tell me anything about the dog?" I asked.

"Auralee's collie, Nana, went everywhere with her. For Christmas, Auralee made her a little red collar with jingle bells on it. I watched from the window as Nicholas set out down the lane. Nana was running ahead of the sleigh; then she stopped and waited for them to catch up."

"And Nana never came home?"

"I never saw her again. I didn't expect to. Not without Auralee."

She looked toward *Dark Sleigh Ride*. The painted collie was just as Grace has described her. Not running but at a standstill in the lane, waiting for the sleigh.

The collie and Nova shared the same markings, which wasn't unusual. White blaze, full white collar, the color of taffy freshly made.

"Collies are loyal," I said, thinking of Nova's attachment to Brent.

Grace nodded. "I'm sure Nana suffered the same fate as the rest of them, whatever that was."

Seeing the glisten of tears in her eyes, I said, "Are you still painting, Grace?"

"I'll always be a painter, but unfortunately, my hands are giving out. That happens at my age. I love to capture the beauty of our countryside in all seasons. I especially like the scenery around Frost Lake. Have you seen our lake?"

"No. Is it far?"

"Less than a mile to the north."

"I'll drive out that way sometime."

"But not when it snows," Grace said. "Call me superstitious, but I make it a point to stay inside when it's snowing. Home is best."

~ * ~

Although I hadn't learned anything new from Grace Allemand, I felt as if I had. She was a link to the decades-old mystery. In her view, the sleigh tragedy might have happened last week. On Christmas Eve.

As I headed home, a strong desire to bring closure to Grace added itself to my many reasons for wanting to solve the mystery of the phantom sleigh.

I also felt that I had made a new friend. In a sense, Grace reminded me of Lucy Hazen, living in a world she immortalized in oil rather than with words. Grace had invited me to return for a visit anytime, whether or not I had anything to report on the sleigh.

She surprised me by quoting a line from a little-known poem by Robert Frost: *a ghost of sleigh bells in a ghost of snow…*

"That's how I picture it," she confided. "Sometimes I hear sleigh bells and I think they're coming home at last, but nothing's there."

Or perhaps she was hearing real bells from one of the modern-day sleighs in the area.

She had a second surprise for me, a Christmas present wrapped in candy cane striped paper.

"Since you love my little sleigh painting, I want you to have a companion piece," she said. "It's a view of Frost Lake in the winter. I took a picture of the lake after a heavy snowfall one year and transferred the scene to canvas."

Relieved that it wasn't another rendering of the doomed sleigh, I unwrapped the package and found a scene of matchless beauty. Frost Lake—all white and silver and palest blue. A surface as smooth as glass with isles of snow that seemed to float as if shaken into motion by a wind. And in the background rose the dark brooding woods of a virgin forest.

"This is breathtaking," I said. "I feel like I'm right there in the picture. I can feel the cold, like it drifts out of the scene. Are you sure you want me to have this?"

"I'm sure. When you look at it, maybe you'll think about me."

"I won't need a reminder, Grace, but thank you so much. I assure you I'll cherish it."

And nothing in the painting would remind Crane of the phantom sleigh.

Later, in the warmth of my car, I shivered, thinking not about Grace or the painting, but about the bells she claimed to have heard. In most circumstances, I loved the sound of bells ringing, but not now, definitely not now, when they were certain to accompany the sleigh.

But I did hear them before I'd driven a mile. My heart raced as I listened. Sleigh bells so sharp and clear they cut deep into the frigid air. Coming closer…Growing louder…

Quickly, I steered my car to the side but saw there was no need. The lane was wide enough for two vehicles.

A sleigh rounded the curve. I saw the horses first, then the passengers. Four young children, red-cheeked and bundled up in contemporary outerwear, possibly middle school students on their winter break. An elderly bewhiskered man drove the sleigh. He waved to me, and I recognized Horace Larkin who emerged from retirement in the winter to conduct various holiday tours.

"Merry Christmas! Happy New Year!" he shouted, and the children echoed the greeting.

It was one of Fred Farmer's sleighs-for-hire, no doubt. I smiled and waved back.

The sleigh passed, and I breathed more easily. For a moment, I'd been afraid that talking about the sleigh with Grace Allemand had somehow summoned it.

But then, another sighting would hardly happen in that way.

Thirty

Brent and Nova were waiting for me in my living room. Julia had served Brent a sandwich and root beer. On his right side, Misty and Sky lay at his feet in begging mode, while Nova kept a wary eye on them from the left.

The rest of my collies circled happily around me, giving me the exuberant greeting they usually reserved for Brent or for Crane when he came home after his long shift.

"Did you learn anything from Grace Allemand?" Julia asked as I hung my parka in the closet.

"Bits and pieces. Nothing earth-shattering."

"Tell us about them," Brent said.

In my retelling, I emphasized the role of the collie. "Auralee raised Nana from a puppy. Nana went everywhere with her."

"Even to her death," Julia murmured.

"I assume so."

"She was like Nova then," Brent said. "A velcro collie. She's always right by my side."

"Nova...Nana," Julia said. "Both start with 'N,' both have two syllables, accent on the first; and they look alike. Is that a coincidence?"

"You're not suggesting that Nova is a reincarnation of Nana, I hope, because that would be weird."

"Here's what's weird," Brent said. "Red Clifton's wife, Ava, came to the barn today looking for Nova. She tried to feed treats to Nova, but I stopped her. I train my dogs not to accept food from strangers. Besides, they were a brand I never heard of."

"How did Nova act around her?" I asked.

"Friendly, like she is with everyone. Not like a dog seeing her first owner again."

"What did she want?"

"The same as her husband. To take Nova home with her."

He set his plate on the floor, and Misty gobbled what was left of the sandwich, rudely nudging Sky out of the way.

"I did some investigating," Brent said. "It was a man who found Nova lying at the side of the road and took her to the shelter. Ava must have abandoned her in the middle of nowhere."

"So she lied. She's lying about her child's illness, too, I'll bet."

"She said she could probably find another collie to pass off as Nova, but her kid might know the difference."

"What a lowlife! Of course he would. I've never seen this Ava, but I detest her."

"She offered me a hundred dollars, cash, for Nova. She said that Kenneth had a sad Christmas, but having Nova back would make it easier for him to go through chemo."

"Maybe she's telling the truth," Julia said.

"I feel certain she isn't."

How did I know this? Perhaps because of her blatant appeal to emotion. Who isn't moved at the thought of a child suffering from cancer?

"I offered to visit Kenneth to cheer him up," Brent said. "A man I know has a litter of collie puppies. I said I'd take one to Kenneth as a gift."

"What did she say to that?"

"That she didn't have time to housebreak a puppy, what with trips to the hospital and all. Nova was older and trained. I told her she couldn't have Nova. That made her mad. She said, 'We'll just see about that' and took off."

How unwise to threaten Brent. He wouldn't be intimidated and certainly didn't need a hundred dollars.

Julia rose. "I'll make us some tea. Brent, would you like another sandwich?"

"Thanks, I'm good, but if you have any Christmas cookies left…"

"Tons of them," I said.

Misty and Candy trotted after her to the kitchen while Sky and Nova remained with Brent.

"We need to figure out why this woman is so determined to get her hands on Nova," I said. "She abandons a dog, then moves heaven and earth to get her back. By the way, how did she know you had Nova? That information is supposed to be confidential."

"There's a new volunteer at the shelter," Brent said, "I found out she gave Ava my address."

"That should never ever happen. I hope you reported her."

"I didn't want to get her in trouble. I can handle it from here."

"You're too good," I said. "Giving out adopters' contact information can lead to all sorts of problems."

"I told her that."

Julia returned with cookies on a dessert plate, along with a silver teapot on a tray and two dainty bone china cups. I'd have preferred a large, hardy mug, but after all it was a holiday week.

"What are you going to do about these people?" Julia asked.

"I'll protect Nova from them. Whatever it takes."

"Do you have a guard at your barn?"

"All the guys know about the situation. They have rifles, mostly if coyotes go after my animals. Nova and Chance come home with me at night."

The hot tea and a moment of reflection worked their magic. "I have an idea. All you're hearing is what they're telling you. If you visit Kenneth, you can take a toy with you. His mother won't have to housebreak that."

"You'll have to find out how old Kenneth is," Julia pointed out. "Also what his interests are."

"I can try. I'll do it."

I frowned, hoping for a stray epiphany. "It's a mystery to me why they want Nova."

"That's for sure," Brent said. "Maybe you can solve it for me."

~ * ~

Toward evening, a light snow began to fall. While Crane turned the pages of the *Banner* quietly, I read a Gothic novel set at the turn of the (old) century. Julia gazed out the window.

"Mother Nature is getting it right this year," she said. "Every day a little new snow to freshen the landscape. It's going to a beautiful day for Brent's New Year's Eve party."

Julia knew that I planned to stay home and wait for Crane.

"I wish you were going," she said. "It's just dinner."

I'd have thought Crane was absorbed in the sports page, but he looked up and said, "You should go, honey. Brent will look after you till I get there."

"Look after me?" I echoed. "Why on earth...?"

"I'll join you when my shift's over," he said quickly.

"We'll see," I said.

But I'd made up my mind to wait for the stroke of midnight at home with Crane. Meeting him at the Hunt Club Inn wasn't the same as going with him.

"Think prime rib," Julia said. "You won't have to cook that day."

In any event, I didn't plan to. I was going to repeat Christmas Day's menu of ham and potato salad with fresh rye bread and a fruit cake.

"It's your decision," Julia said, "but I'd never pass up a champagne dinner at the Hunt Club Inn." She rose. "I'm going to turn in."

Crane folded the paper and moved the leftover cookies out of Candy's reach.

"Are you familiar with the Frost Lake area?" I asked.

"Sure. There isn't much there, just fancy houses and woods. Why?"

"I'd like to see the scene that inspired our new painting. Grace told me not to go when it's snowing. I think she doesn't like to drive in the winter."

"I wish more people felt that way. We'd have fewer accidents. There are some treacherous curves around the lake" he added.

"I'll wait for better weather."

"Where do you think we should hang the new painting?" he asked.

"I don't know. The walls on this floor are full. How about in the hall upstairs?"

"That'll work."

In between my office and the guest room. And every time I'd pass it, I would think about the haunted sleigh and remember this strange Christmas.

Grace might as well have painted the sleigh in the picture, for my lively imagination had already placed it there.

Thirty-one

Begin the new year doing what you hope to do all year.

I recalled that sage advice as I dressed the next morning. I had made my decision. At the stroke of midnight I would be in my fireplace-warmed home with my husband and our collie family.

Ring out the old, ring in the new.

With bells? I slid over the image of bells clanging in the cold winter air. We were still in the holiday season—the twelve days of Christmas. No evil thing had the power to touch me. Not that the lost sleigh riders were evil, but...

Enough!

If Crane and I were to celebrate New Year's Eve in style, I needed to add a few festive decorations to the house and buy supplies. Popcorn, champagne, paper bells, horns, and perhaps a holiday movie.

That would entail a quick trip to Blackbourne's Grocers, and I might as well leave now before the day's snow arrived.

The dogs gathered around me as I changed into my tall boots. They anticipated a walk, although they knew only three of them would go with me. To their dismay, no one did. I pulled up the hood of my purple parka, wound my scarf around my neck, and set out for the grocery store with instructions to them to watch the house and Julia who was still sleeping.

"We'll go for a walk when I get home," I said.

Blackbourne's parking lot was crowded with people who had the same idea of laying in party supplies. I cruised through the lot twice before I found a place to park.

Inside, the checkout lanes were longer than I'd ever seen them. Undaunted, I headed for the party section and gathered enough decorations to rival the Hunt Club Inn, including packages of silver paper bells.

"Hey, Jennet! Happy New Year!"

Molly, my young friend from Sagramore Lake Road, and her constant companion, Jennifer, wheeled their cart in my direction. It was full of baking supplies. How they had grown! When I'd met them, they were little girls selling lemonade and homemade cookies.

"Are you having a New Year's party?" Jennifer asked.

I dropped the bells into my basket. "I'm just dressing up the house for the holiday. Was Santa good to you girls?"

"Very good," Molly said. "My mom and dad gave me a digital camera."

"I got ice skates," Molly said. "Now I can join the Ice Spinners."

The name was self-explanatory. Still, I asked, "Is that a club?"

"Not officially. It's a group of kids from high school. They go ice skating every week."

"It sounds like fun."

"I'm still an amateur," Molly said. "My ankles hurt when I skate and sometimes I fall."

"Now *that* doesn't sound like fun."

"I'll get better," she added. "Jennifer already skates like a pro."

"Stop over before school starts," I said. "Santa left something for you two under the tree. There's something for Ginger, too."

They promised to do so, wished me a happy new year again, and I joined one of the long lines, glad I'd remembered to pick up books for the girls at the Green House of Antiques and wrapped a box of Camille's fresh baked dog treats for Ginger.

Yes, it was still Christmastime.

~ * ~

While I'd been in the store, the snow had started, light flakes that promised to cover the tire tracks and related grime that marred the parking lot.

What a perfect holiday season!

Under the new layer of snow, the road had acquired a thin sheen of ice. Mindful of black ice, I slowed to the annoyance of drivers behind me who were cruising along as if it were still summer. A horn blasted, then another. Somebody shouted a rude comment.

Ahead, I spied a lesser traveled by-road that would take me only about ten minutes out of my way. It was a scenic route, winding through farmland and stretches of wood with Deer X-ing signs posted at intervals. These didn't worry me.

Dawn and dusk were usually prime times for wandering deer, and it was long past dawn. But 'usually' is relative. I kept my eyes glued to the road. Suddenly—I didn't know why—I was anxious to return to my more familiar route home.

Far away, bells began to ring. Wasn't there a church nearby in a very small town with a population of about five hundred? I thought so.

They aren't sleigh bells. They're church bells. Ringing in the early afternoon? For a funeral?

They grew louder. And louder.

Please let it be one of Fred Farmer's sleighs, I prayed.

In seconds, the light snowfall thickened. Visibility plummeted.

Get out of its way! I told myself and stepped on the gas pedal.

The road was narrower than most, the verge overgrown with dead growth draped in white. I didn't have much room. No matter. I had to move.

I heard the singer then, his rich baritone blending with the clanging bells.

Now the holly bears the berry as green as the grass,
And Mary bore Jesus who died on the cross,
And Mary bore Jesus, our savior for to be...

So loud was the singer's voice that he might have been sitting next to me in the car.

I pulled over as far as I could until the young trees at the woods' edge brushed against the side of the Ford.

And waited. The song came to an abrupt stop.

I saw the sleigh, saw it clearly, and didn't think to question how I could do so through the falling snow.

~ * ~

"I think I know where we are," Nicholas shouted.

Margaret leaned forward, her hand on his shoulder, her soft voice barely audible.

"Are we near the Hall?"

He didn't answer.

"Nicholas will take us there," Edmund said.

Auralee spoke. "It's so cold. I'm freezing. I can't feel my fingers."

"Don't think about it," Edmund said. "Let's sing."

"It isn't helping," Margaret said.

Edmund ignored her. "All of you, sing with me. The words are in the songbook."

He continued the carol:

Now the holly bears the berry as black as the coal,

And Mary bore Jesus who died for us all...

"Coal and all don't rhyme," Auralee said. Her voice trembled. "I just want to go home. Are you telling us the truth, Nicholas? We're lost, aren't we? We're going to die."

Although she'd claimed she couldn't feel her fingers, she reached inside her coat and pulled out her silver necklace, holding it as if it were a talisman.

Again, Nicholas didn't answer. He guided the sleigh onto a by-road. Almost immediately everything—horses, sleigh, riders— dissipated in a snow squall. They were gone. They might never have passed my way.

Still, strangely, I heard a dog barking. Nana? But couldn't see her.

~ * ~

I sat in the car, attempting to regain my equilibrium. I had been swept into the sleigh riders' world again, which was why I could hear their exchanges so clearly and see their sleigh through the falling snow. Had it really disappeared or had Nicholas taken it through the snow squall? Was he even now driving the horses down another country lane?

For a moment, I toyed with the idea of following it. Of finding out what was going on once and for all.

But I promptly rejected all thoughts of overtaking the sleigh. I couldn't very well follow a supernatural manifestation. Well, maybe in some circumstances I could, but where would that leave me? In a twilight world where the snow was forever, and rest everlasting was an impossible dream?

As soon I as felt calm enough to drive, I continued on my way, eventually returning to my regular route, and made my way to Jonquil Lane. Safely home. And all the way, the words of the Sans Day carol played in my mind:

Now the holly bears the berry as blood it is red,
And Mary bore Jesus who rose from the dead...

~ * ~

I told Julia about my encounter with the sleigh as I unloaded my purchases. She was having a light breakfast of raisin toast and tea. Now that I was engaged in a mundane task in familiar surroundings, the sleigh and the snow squall acquired a veneer of unreality.

"I should have been with you," Julia said.

"You were sleeping," I pointed out. "This is your vacation. There was no need for you to go grocery shopping with me."

The tea was tepid. Craving a hot drink, I put more water on to boil and spooned fresh leaves into the teapot.

Would the sleigh have materialized if Julia had been sitting beside me in the passenger's seat? I'd never know.

"I'm missing out on all the fun," Julia said.

"I wouldn't call it fun. The riders are lost. It's freezing. The girls are frightened. Edmund is trying to keep their spirits up by singing."

"I want to know what happens before I go home, Julia said. "And I want you to be safe."

"So do I," I said. "I have a feeling I'll see the sleigh again. It has a story to tell, and it hasn't reached the end yet."

Thirty-two

Later that day, Brent sat in the kitchen crumbling a Christmas cookie while Candy and Nova fixed their soulful eyes on the dessert plate. Misty had lapped up the green sugar that had spilled on the floor, thereby losing her place at Brent's feet.

He put a tiny piece in his mouth. "You're not going to believe what happened. I can hardly believe it myself."

"Tell us," Julia said.

"I just had a visit from the law. Apparently, Ava has accused me of sexual harassment. She claims I fondled her."

"You?" I almost spilled the coffee I was pouring in his cup.

"Yes, me. Like I need to seduce a woman, especially one who's out to steal my dog."

He was so indignant, so serious, that I fought back the urge to laugh. Instead, I said, "What does that have to do with her wanting Nova back for her sick kid?"

"Not a damn thing."

"How did it come about?" Julia asked.

"She came out to the barn again to ask me if I'd reconsidered about letting her take Nova. I never gave her any reason to think I would. I offered to visit Kenneth to cheer him up, like we talked about.

"She turned me down and said something like if she didn't have Nova when she left, I was going to be very sorry. I shouted at her to get off my property."

I said, "You told all this to the officer, I assume."

"Yes, and everything that went on before, how she tried to give me a hundred dollars for Nova. Now she claims I dragged her into my office..."

"To have your way with her?" Julia couldn't suppress her mirth at the outrageous scene he painted. "What does she look like?"

"Blonde like you. Sort of pretty. I never touched her."

"How did she manage to escape your clutches?" I asked.

"She said Nova growled at me, and I let her go."

"That's funny," Julia said. "Nova growling at you, that is. She'd never do that."

He glared at her. "It isn't funny to me."

"Do you have any witnesses?" I wanted to know.

Brent looked at me as if I'd insulted him.

"Just Nova. My word has always been good enough."

"For us, yes, but this policeman doesn't know you."

"It would be helpful if someone besides Nova heard your exchange," Julia pointed out.

"Well, they didn't. I had three guys working at the barn, and no one noticed anything except raised voices. What's worse, she's going to give her story to the press."

"Oh, no!"

"She isn't going to give up. I'm keeping an eagle eye on Nova. I never have trouble getting women interested in me," he added oblivious of how conceited that sounded.

"I wonder why her husband didn't come with her," I said.

Brent shrugged. "I don't know. You'd think two against one would be more effective, looking at it through their eyes."

"Where do you stand now?" I asked.

"Let her file a complaint. She doesn't have any proof, and I don't have anything to hide."

"That's best. Don't sink to her level."

Brent stared at the mess he'd made on the table. "Any chance I can get some more cookies, Jennet?"

"Every chance." I opened a pretty tin with a gingerbread house on the lid. "These are Camille's. They're fancier than mine."

He seemed calmer, still indignant at being unjustly accused but ready to do battle with Ava. As for myself, I still couldn't imagine why Nova was so important to Ava and her husband. More than ever I doubted the veracity of her story about Kenneth. He probably didn't exist.

~ * ~

The next morning, Julia and I set out to visit Lucy at Dark Gables. Brent's dilemma had provided me with a minimum of distraction, but since my encounter with the sleigh on the way home from Blackbourne's Grocers, most of my thoughts centered on the long-ago plight of the four riders.

If they were traveling up and down the roads and lanes of Foxglove Corners, in and out of snow squalls and storms, other people sensitive to the world beyond must have seen them. Edwina Endicott, for example.

With only two days remaining until New Year's Eve, I resolved to carve out time to go to the library. If Edwina wasn't there, somewhere I had her card.

I turned off Spruce Road and drove slowly up Lucy's well-shaded driveway.

"How do you think Lucy can help?" Julia asked.

"I'm not sure," I said. "If nothing else she can read my tea leaves."

"But you don't believe in that," she said. "Do you?"

"Sometimes. Lucy would be the first to tell me to take her foretellings with a grain of salt. But she's different from most people. She has remarkable talents. You have to *believe*," I said. "It's like... Let's see...She can tune into the other world and bring back a report of what's going to happen to you in the future."

"I'll withhold judgment, but I sure hope she can suggest something."

I nodded, even though Julia was looking out of the window and couldn't see me.

"Something other than waiting," I said.

I glanced at the thick forest of leafless hardwoods and brooding spruces that lined the driveway to Dark Gables. It was easy to imagine the very trees whispering, *Abandon all hope ye who enter here.*

Suppose at this very moment, the phantom sleigh emerged from the lane that ran along the west side of the house? Suppose we were once again on a collision course?

"This has to be the gloomiest house I've ever seen," Julia said. "Even with the holiday decorations."

Lucy dressed as she imagined a horror writer would, usually in black dresses with gold jewelry. Her favorite piece was a bracelet of Zodiac charms that jingled when she moved her arm. Today, she had thrown an ivory shawl over her shoulders.

She was expecting us, and her blue merle collie was overjoyed to have company.

"Julia. How nice! And Jennet. I was hoping to see you before the old year ends," she said. "Did you ever see the sleigh again?"

"I did, just this morning. I have to admit it has me spooked."

"As well it should."

"Why do you say that?" Julia asked while I braced myself for a heady dose of gloom and doom.

"I had a premonition," she said. "Danger is thickening all around you, Jennet. It's going to be difficult for you to prevail, but you will. I'm pretty sure you will."

"'Pretty sure' isn't very encouraging."

"Does this danger come from the sleigh?" Julia asked.

"Not exactly. I don't think so. The danger originates in an unexpected place. It's all murky." She added, "Let's have tea. Maybe the leaves will be more specific."

She escorted us to the sunroom in the back of the house where she brought her tales of vampires and zombies to life. While she prepared the tea, I described the morning's encounter with the supernatural.

"I heard sleigh bells, and the sleigh materialized on this lonely country road. I heard the riders talking. It was snowing and so cold. Nicholas, who was driving the sleigh, was lost. Edmund was trying to keep their spirits up by singing."

"Many parts of Foxglove Corners were a wilderness in 1937," Lucy said. "That's true even today. So what do we have? Four people lost in a snowstorm, but they have transportation, the horse-drawn sleigh. We know they never came home."

"They were lost indeed," I said. "Lost in time. They had a collie with them, Nana."

I tended to forget her, possibly because I didn't always see her, even though the collie had been part of the excursion.

"I don't understand how all traces of a large sleigh containing four people can vanish," Julia said. "I'd think there'd be some trace of it. Somewhere."

The teakettle whistled. Lucy brought three plain white cups out of the kitchen, then opened a package of gingerbread cookies. Sky's ears shot up.

"I don't understand that, either," Lucy said, "but I think I know what your role is, Jennet. You're the finder."

Thirty-three

While Lucy read Julia's tea leaves, amusing her with news of an impending engagement, I brooded over Lucy's words.

I was the finder? Didn't I have any say in the matter? And what was I expected to do? Search every inch of Foxglove Corners, including the countless acres of woods?

It troubled me that Lucy had also spoken of danger without assuring me that, ultimately, I would be victorious. This was the first of my mysteries in which no villain lurked in the sidelines. I certainly didn't view the lost sleigh riders as antagonists.

The first time I'd seen the sleigh, however, it had come close to ending my life.

Think about that.

Lucy was showing Julia a light tea leaf shaped like a tiny heart. Incredibly, Julia was blushing. "There's no engagement in my future," she insisted.

"The leaves say otherwise."

Sky had been patient long enough. She aimed her mouth at the cookie Julia had been holding in her hand as if to say, *If you don't want it, give it to me.*

"Is it all right if she has one?" she asked.

"Perfectly. There's nothing in it that could harm her."

"What am I supposed to do?" I asked. "Follow the sleigh the next time I see it? I thought about doing that today."

"Why didn't you?" Lucy asked.

I cast my mind back to those moments. "It drove off into a snow squall. I thought it disappeared."

In retrospect, I should have followed it. What kind of sleuth was I? Even if I found myself on an empty road. Oh, yes. I remembered now. "I thought it was futile to try to catch a supernatural apparition."

"No doubt it is." Lucy set Julia's cup on the wicker coffee table. I leaned closer to study the formations on the white china surface. To me the leaf in question did look like a heart. A mini-Valentine.

"Weren't you seeing an English professor at the college, Julia?" I asked.

"Off and on. We're certainly not an item."

"Give it time," Lucy said. "The teacup knows. And Jennet, the sleigh will pass by you again, and you'll know what to do. I have faith in you."

What I needed was faith in myself. At the moment, all I could feel was apprehension.

~ * ~

Julia said, "I'd rather go for a walk than to the library. Which dogs should I take with me?"

I didn't have to think about that. "Halley and Sky. They're the gentlest."

While she set out down the lane with the chosen two, I searched my desk for Edwina's card in case she wasn't at the library. I couldn't find it, but fortunately, a little later, I found Edwina herself in the Gothic Nook, filling a basket with aging paperbacks and nibbling on a chocolate marshmallow bell.

"Hello, Edwina," I said. "I was hoping to run into you today."

This was something I'd never said to her. Her eyes lit up. "Did you see a ghost?"

"Seven of them, including three animals."

"You are *so* lucky." She sat in one of the vintage chairs and set her basket on the floor. "Tell me all about it."

"I've seen a phantom sleigh traveling on the roads of Foxglove Corners."

"I knew you were keeping a secret!"

When I'd filled in all the details, she asked, "Are you sure it wasn't one of Fred Farmer's sleighs? I've seen them from time to time."

I'd thought my story had made it clear that my sleigh was an apparition. Apparently not.

"It was real," I said. "A real apparition, I mean."

"Then you must be seeing those people who vanished in the nineteen-thirties."

"I'm sure you're right."

"Were they on Huron Court?"

That was the road on which the unsuspecting traveler experienced an abrupt change of seasons along with a trip backward or forward in time. Both Edwina and I had seen the spirit of Violet Randall and her dog walking on Huron Court.

"I've seen the sleigh on various roads in Foxglove Corners. Did you ever see it?"

She shook her head. "Sadly, no. I'd give anything to add it to my sightings, though. You say you could hear the people talking?"

"As clearly as I'm hearing you, even though I was in my car the whole time."

"Well, then, you know what happened to them."

"They haven't shown me that yet. All I know is they lost their way in a snowstorm."

"They could be anywhere then." Edwina unwrapped another marshmallow bell from the candy dish. "Have one. They're delicious."

I didn't need any further encouragement. Miss Eidt always had the best chocolates. "If the riders were somehow separated from the sleigh, yes. I don't imagine Nicholas could steer the sleigh into the woods."

"Nicholas?" she echoed.

"Their names match the ones in the news story. Auralee, Margaret, Edmund, and Nicholas."

"Just think, Jennet," Edwina said. "You could be the one to solve an old mystery."

"If I see the sleigh again," I added.

You will.

For a moment, I thought Edwina had uttered the words, but the whisper was in my head.

"I'm so jealous," Edwina said. "My little apparition pales beside yours."

"What did you see?" I asked.

"A collie running loose on Cherrytree Lane. I thought it was real until it vanished right before my eyes."

"A ghost dog," I murmured.

"It looked like Lassie. At first, I thought it was Violet's dog. I still think that."

"Cherrytree Lane is a long way from Huron Court," I pointed out.

"That's right, but dogs get around, even if they're spirit dogs. After all, they have four legs."

"I don't think Violet's collie would leave her side," I said. "This had to be another dog."

Another stray set adrift to make its own way in the wilderness? I'd have to drive down Cherrytree Lane and see if I could rescue it. But Edwina was convinced she'd seen a ghost dog.

"I saw him vanish," she said. "What I especially remember is this ghost dog wore a wide red collar with jingle bells on it. I heard them ringing even after it disappeared."

Nana!

Thank heavens I'd confided in Edwina. She hadn't seen the sleigh, but part of the apparition had showed itself to her.

"You saw Nana, the dog who ran with the sleigh," I said.

Edwina's eyes grew brighter still. "I did?"

"Her name was Nana. She was Auralee's collie. Like Violet's dog, she went everywhere with her, even on that last sleigh ride."

"But I didn't see the sleigh."

"Nana must have left the sleigh," I mused. "But why? You saw her on Cherrytree Lane?"

"I was driving around, looking at Christmas decorations when I saw a dog in the road. She was only there for a minute, then she sort of dissipated."

I helped myself to another marshmallow bell and thought about a spirit dog wandering through the wilds of Foxglove Corner, the jingle bells on her collar sending their tinkling music out into the winter air.

I imagined that Nana, like any dog, might have wandered away from the sleigh, following a delicious scent. Then she'd find her way back to it.

As soon as I got home, I intended to sketch a rough map of Foxglove Corners and trace the sleigh's route, based on the places it had been sighted. I wasn't sure how that would help, but it certainly wouldn't hurt.

Thirty-four

An hour later, I had a hand-drawn map on which I'd pasted silver stars over the phantom sleigh's known routes. In other words, wherever I'd seen it. First was Windemere, where I'd been forced off the road; then on that narrow by-road near Blackbourne's Groceries. Suppressing a shiver, I pasted a star on Jonquil Lane, and one on Cherrytree Lane where Edwina had sighted Nana.

Could the sleigh have been in the vicinity, only hidden from Edwina's view? It was possible. It was equally possible it wouldn't hide itself from me.

All right. Cherrytree Lane. I'd never been in that area but knew it was mostly woods, hills, and lakes. I sat back and examined my work. All it proved was that Nicholas had covered most of Foxglove Corners as he searched through driving snow for the road that would take him and his friends home.

Why had he never found the way back to Faraday Hall?

I closed my eyes and let my imagination create a scene that remained in the bittersweet realm of If Only.

The four weary riders and Nana bursting through the front door of Faraday Hall, covered with snow and half frozen. Nicholas blustery and triumphant at having brought his party safe home. Auralee pale, her blonde hair laced with snowdrops, still shaking uncontrollably, and clutching her precious necklace as if to make sure it was still there. Margaret, her face reddened by the wind and cold, moving swiftly toward the fireplace. Edmund singing the last verse of the Sans Day carol while Nana shook her coat vigorously.

I could see everything with a clarity that bordered on the unnatural. In the massive living room, a tall balsam fir tree with real candles on its branches. A table laden with wine and plates of thinly-sliced fruit cake. A pitcher of eggnog. Chairs drawn up to a fireplace where flames leaped high.

My fictitious scene faded, but while it had lasted, how real it had seemed.

I'd felt almost as if I were one of the party. As I had been with them in my dream.

Yes. Riding with their skeletons.

Enough fantasizing. I pushed that last gruesome memory away. In a short while, I'd gone from joyous to morbid.

Julia came tripping downstairs with Candy at her heels. "What are you doing, Jennet?" she asked.

"Making a map. Would you like to go for a ride with me?"

"Now? It's almost dinnertime."

I glanced at the clock, surprised to see that I had been poring over my map and fantasies for almost two hours.

"So it is. Tomorrow morning then."

"Where are we going?"

"In search of a ghost dog," I said. "It seems I'm not the only one seeing spirits this winter."

~ * ~

Cherrytree Lane was far from the wilderness I had envisioned. Pricey mansions sat on hills amid expertly maintained landscaping. The lakes we'd passed so far were ornamental, possibly man-made, and the woods had been thinned, trees felled to make way for palatial dwellings, enough left to provide atmosphere.

A sign swam by in a swirl of snow flurries. Cherrytree Estates.

Of course. Edwina wouldn't have been on a Christmas decoration tour in a wilderness. But in 1937, the area would have been largely untouched. A pristine paradise.

"I don't think we're going to see your ghost dog today," Julia said. "But I'm glad I came. The scenery is spectacular."

"I didn't think I would. Spirits show themselves at their discretion. I just wanted to see the road where Edwina saw Nana."

"Do you think she really did?" Julia asked. "You used to think Edwina Endicott was an airhead."

"She described Nana's red jingle bell collar and the way she vanished. So, yes, she saw part of the apparition, not all of it."

I was convinced Edwina had seen the dog who ran with the sleigh, although admittedly a red collar with jingle bells attached was hardly unique at this time of year.

Julia turned away from the window. "All this snow! I'm craving a cup of hot chocolate with marshmallows and whipped cream and maybe green and red sugar on top. The works."

She painted an enticing picture. "All that? Your cup would run over."

"I'll ask for an extra-large cup."

"Let's stop at Clovers then," I said. "Annica's working today. They'll be closed for New Year's Day."

I turned the car around and headed toward Crispian Road and Clovers. How much easier navigation was in the twenty-first century, and when it wasn't snowing heavily.

For a moment, I thought I heard sleigh bells ringing out in the snowy countryside. But the road was untraveled, the flurries light, and the silence was unbroken.

~ * ~

Annica set three cups of cocoa on the table and joined us. Julia's drink was as elaborate as she could have wished. I set the miniature marshmallows into a spin around my cup and took a sip. Hot and delicious.

"Business is pathetic," Annica said. "Mary Jeanne's closing early. I'm going shopping for a new dress to wear tomorrow night."

All of Annica's dresses looked new to me, always bright and elegantly designed, flattering her figure and her red-gold hair.

She took a sip of her cocoa. "I'm looking for a green dress to go with my emeralds. It has to be perfect. It's going to be a perfect night." She took another sip and abruptly changed the subject. "What can we do to help Brent through this latest crisis?"

"You mean with that ludicrous sexual harassment accusation?" I asked.

She nodded. "That awful woman. Why would she target Brent?"

"Let's not miss the point," I said. "It's about Nova. For some reason, she wants the dog, and she's desperate enough to go to any lengths to get her."

"That doesn't make any sense. There's nothing special about Nova. She isn't Lassie, for heaven's sake."

"She was in a shelter," Julia pointed out. "Anyone who qualified could have adopted her."

"And Nova was there because Ava abandoned her," I said. "If we believe the story. You can't trust a liar to tell the truth."

"Brent has really taken this to heart," Annica said. "He's a good, honorable man. Besides, nobody likes to be accused of something he didn't do. Especially something like that. I wonder if she's hoping for a cash settlement."

I considered that briefly. "I don't think money has anything to do with it, but I don't know."

"We have to help him," Annica said.

"Offhand, I don't know what we can do."

"She threatened to go to the press with her story. I didn't see anything in the *Banner* yet."

"You won't," I said. "It was an idle threat. It's bad enough there's a police report on file."

"Look on it as a mystery, Jennet," Annica said. "You're the sleuth. If it's all about Nova, let's start with her. Can you find out the name of the shelter she was in?"

"Brent will know."

"Ask him. Then we can visit it together and see if we can fill in Nova's background. That's if there's more to the story than Ava not wanting to be bothered with taking care of a dog."

"We can do that, but it'll have to wait until after the holiday," I said. "Maybe the volunteer who gave out Brent's contact information will know something about Ava."

"It's a plan, then," Annica said. "Let's wrap this mystery up and start the new year on a positive note."

I took the last sip of cocoa and promptly decided to order another cup.

"Let's wrap up the phantom sleigh mystery, too," she added.

"Before I go home," Julia said.

Thirty-five

I hung the last paper bell on the chandelier above the dining room table and stepped carefully down from the stool, sending my helpers, Misty and Velvet, scurrying back to the kitchen. They suffered from a baseless fear of getting stepped on.

Everything was ready for the quiet, private celebration I planned to have with Crane: a semi-boneless ham, potato salad in the refrigerator, a bottle of champagne, a plate of cookies, and a lemon meringue pie.

And bells. The good kind that looked pretty but wouldn't ring and usher in a phantom sleigh.

A deep silence pervaded the house. Julia was upstairs planning her wardrobe for Brent's New Year's Eve dinner later today, and the other collies were sleeping the lazy winter afternoon away. Misty and Velvet lay close together in front of the fireplace like the good friends they were.

I felt oddly at peace, as if the danger had passed, leaving me unscathed. I told myself the phantom sleigh was a holiday manifestation, and, as of midnight, holiday time was over.

Not quite. Remember the twelve days of Christmas.

But that was just a song. No one in the modern world celebrated Christmas for twelve days, did they?

Never ever let your guard down.

A light rap on the front door woke the collies. Alert and noisy, they converged in the vestibule. I glanced out the window, half expecting to see Brent's vintage Plymouth in the driveway, but it wasn't there. Two sets of fresh boot prints marred the walkway.

The rap sounded again, giving rise to a renewed barking frenzy.

I opened the door to Molly and Jennifer, bundled up in parkas and scarves and rosy cheeked. Jennifer held a Christmas-wrapped package in mittened hands. I'd almost forgotten my earlier invitation.

"Happy New Year!" they said in unison.

"We brought you a present." Molly held the box above the bobbing collie heads.

I issued a stern command to sit and stay, but the girls didn't mind being set upon. They loved collies. In fact, I might well be looking at the next generation of collie rescuers.

I took their jackets and told them to keep their boots on as we all, people and dogs, tracked in snow on the rug. Molly took off her mittens and shoved them in her pocket. They were black with blue and pink threaded into the fabric, a match for her scarf.

"What's in the box?" I asked.

"Christmas cookies," Jennifer said. "I guess you could call them New Year's cookies."

More cookies. Oh well, you could never have too many. They'd soon disappear, and I'd have to bake again.

"How lovely," I said. "Did you make them yourselves?"

"With Mom's cookie press," Jennifer said. "They're all snowflakes."

I brought their presents out from under the tree. I'd bought them books, a vintage series book for each, along with *Treve* for Jennifer and *Bruce* for Molly. The girls periodically checked out Albert Payson Terhune books from the library. These they could keep.

Jennifer stared uncertainly at the series book as if it were an alien artifact. To a modern young girl, it probably was.

"I think you'll enjoy these," I said. "A group of girls spend a summer out west where they have a fantastic adventure, and the following summer they crash their plane on an uninhabited island."

They didn't look convinced but made a fuss over the collie books and thanked me profusely.

"Are you girls still skating with the Ice Spinners?" I asked.

"We're going out this afternoon," Molly said.

"On New Year's Eve?"

"Sure," Jennifer said. "Why not? In a few more days, we'll be back in school."

"I see. Take advantage of the good weather. I hear there's a snowstorm on the way for tomorrow."

Jennifer perked up. "Hey! Maybe we'll have a snow day."

"You never know."

I wouldn't mind returning to school a day late myself. Like the old year, Christmas vacation had sped by. For many reasons, I needed more time.

~ * ~

Molly and Jennifer went home, happily chatting about their collie books and ice-skating plans. Julia and I sampled the girls' cookie press snowflakes with cups of steaming tea, after which Julia decided to take a nap.

"I want to be rested for tonight," she said.

"You'll shine," I told her.

I settled in the rocker with Phyllis A. Whitney's *Thunder Heights*, determined to enjoy every minute of one of my last free days in my cozy, warm house. Let the young people skate across a frozen lake in the cold. I saw all the winter I wanted to see through my front window.

And I hoped no one else would come over.

My cell phone's melodious notes broke the spell of Whitney's atmospheric novel. I glanced at the number. Grace Allemand was calling with a wish for a Happy New Year, I hoped. Nothing more.

But it was more. She wasted no time with pleasantries or holiday wishes.

"I saw the ghost sleigh this morning, Jennet," she said. "It passed right in front of my house. I wanted to get dressed and follow it, but I'm in no condition to do that. I had to watch as it went by."

"Are you sure it was the phantom sleigh?" I asked.

"Positive. It had evergreen roping on the sides and red ribbons. I heard the sleigh bells and recognized my aunt and her friends. I even saw Nana. Just like I remembered them on that last day."

She was excited, but I was a trifle doubtful. She had never seen the apparition, not once in all the years since the riders had set out. Why now?

Even while I wondered, I saw a light in the darkness. If Grace had seen the sleigh and Edwina had seen Nana, I wasn't as alone with the manifestation as I'd thought.

But could discussing the sleigh have set Grace's imagination alight? Could she have seen one of Fred Farmer's sleighs-for-hire and peopled it with her lost ones?

I decided to believe her.

"What do you think it means?" she asked.

"Who can know? Maybe the sleigh is reaching the end of its journey."

"I had another thought," she said. "Tell me what you think. Is it possible that the sleigh has come for me?"

"What do you mean?"

"Remember, I told you my aunt said I could go on the sleigh with them the next time."

"You're not talking about death, I hope."

"It crossed my mind."

I took a minute to find the right words to express my thoughts and to suppress the jolt of fear that came out of the blue. A memory rose up in my mind: the sleigh ornament speaking, saying 'Come join us.'

"Death doesn't work that way," I said. "You're not sick, are you?"

"I have a little cold. Nothing serious. But I'm old. I won't be afraid of death if I can be with those I loved."

I didn't like what I was hearing.

"There's a reason we've seen the sleigh, but it isn't a harbinger of death. Of that I'm sure."

"I'm not."

"Well, I've seen it and, sleigh or no sleigh, I don't intend to die any time soon," I said briskly. "I'm young. I have a husband I love, and dogs who depend on me."

After a long pause, she said. "Maybe you're right. I only wish I'd had a longer look at the sleigh. I'd so loved to have seen everyone properly again."

I wished her a happy New Year, ended the call, and sat back to ponder the incident. The ever-in-motion sleigh had been last sighted in the Frost Lake area.

That had to be significant.

Thirty-six

No further interruptions disturbed the peace of the afternoon. I texted Crane, ascertained that he was safe and looking forward to our private celebration.

Julia left early to pick up Annica and Lucy. They were driving to the Hunt Club Inn together, which I thought was a good idea.

Alone except for the dogs, I set the dining room table for two and went upstairs to select my own wardrobe. Crane's favorite red dress, I decided, and my crystal snowflake pendant. What I would have worn to the Hunt Club Inn.

I'd change my clothes later, just before Crane came home.

That left several hours with nothing more pressing to do than walk the dogs. Eventually, I returned to the rocker and *Thunder Heights*, but although the story had captured my attention, I felt my eyelids grow heavy and close. It was too great an effort to force them to stay open.

~ * ~

Through my dreams, sleigh bells went ringing. I woke, every sense on high alert. The discordant music was so loud that the sleigh might have been on Jonquil Lane again, in front of the house.

And that's exactly where it was. In front of the house, a three-dimensional apparition paused not three yards from our walkway. The dark horses stamped restlessly on the snow-packed lane, blowing out puffs of freezing breath. The collie, Nana, had leaped into the sleigh and sat cuddled in Auralee's lap.

Edmund had finished his song and, apparently, wasn't inclined to call for another one. Nana whimpered softly like one of my own dogs. The bells were so loud their tones struck notes of pain in my ears. How could that be when the sleigh wasn't in motion, the horses weren't running?

Once again the riders' features and their voices were clear, heard over the clanging tones of the sleigh bells.

Auralee grasped the silver necklace with one hand; with the other she stroked the collie's head, whispering comforting words to her.

"It's all right, pretty girl. Don't be afraid. I'm here."

Margaret said, "This isn't it, Nicholas. It isn't Faraday Hall."

How could I hear her over the clanging of the bells?

"You're right. Sorry. I thought I had the right road."

"There's a house," Margaret said. "I think. It's all so fuzzy. Maybe it isn't really there. Whoever heard of a green house?"

Nicholas turned toward the house. He appeared to be looking at me. I could see how blue his eyes were.

"It must be a mirage," Edmund said. "But how can four people see the same mirage?"

"Nicholas!" Auralee wailed. "We can't last much longer. Can't you please, please find us a shelter?"

"That house," Nicholas said. "We'll ask if we can stay with them until the storm blows itself out."

Edmund said. "What the...? I don't see it now. Where did it go?"

Margaret wailed. "It's gone. Nicholas, what are we going to do?"

"We'll keep going," Nicholas said. "Otherwise, we're going to die out here."

From somewhere, as from an invisible radio, I heard a sonorous voice. *Danger! Danger! The winter storm is going to arrive earlier than expected. This will be a bad one. Stay off the roads.*

Danger...danger...danger...

Instantly, the light flurries turned into a monster snow squall, and the sleigh vanished.

Jonquil Lane was empty. If I threw on my parka and boots and ventured out to the road, I knew I wouldn't see sleigh tracks or horses' hooves.

I pushed back a wayward strand of hair and ran my hand along my eyes. Where was the sleigh going now?

Nicholas had said they had to keep moving...or die. His words haunted me as did the mention of the fuzzy green house that had appeared in what Edmund called a mirage.

It must have been our house in which he'd thought to seek shelter.

Impossible. The house didn't exist in 1937.

The yellow Victorian was much older, genuinely vintage, and it was right across the lane. Why hadn't the weary travelers seen Camille's house?

The only answer I could think of was chilling. This was my apparition, not Camille's.

The squall had changed back to light flurries. The bells were silent. The voice's echo had faded. If it had ever been. Had it migrated from my dream?

Wait! No! I hadn't been dreaming. The ghost bells had awakened me.

The house was silent now. Velvet still lay in front of the fireplace, the choice resting place in the house, but Misty had risen and followed me to the window. Her soft whine broke the silence.

"Did you see them, girl?" I asked. "Did you hear the ghosts talking?"

She whined again and nudged my hand, fixing me with a soulful collie stare that seemed to say *I saw the other dog and the horses.*

"What's going to happen?" I murmured.

Naturally, there was no answer.

~ * ~

An hour passed. The flurries left a light layer of snow on the land and retreated behind a mass of low-lying gray clouds.

I arranged four pineapple rings on top of the ham and put it in the oven. The potato salad and relish tray were in the refrigerator; the pie cooled on the counter away from eager collie noses and mouths.

Someone was pounding on the front door. The dogs came together in a noisy race to greet or warn away the company. I looked through the widow, again expecting to see Brent's vintage Plymouth parked behind my car.

I didn't recognize the beige SUV in the driveway.

"Back," I ordered and grabbed Candy's collar.

Two women stood on the porch stamping snow from their boots. One was tall, blonde, and swathed in black wool. The other, shorter with dark, silvered hair, had a blue scarf wrapped around her mouth. They were both vaguely familiar. Neighbors, I thought, and found a smile. As the tall one spoke, I remembered them. Jennifer's and Molly's mothers. Their names were Jackie and Mary Lou.

The tall one, Jackie, spoke. "Mrs. Ferguson? I'm so glad you're home. We're looking for Jennifer and Molly. Are they still here?"

"It's Jennet," I said. "Come in. They were here about three hours ago. They brought me a box of cookies, and I gave them their presents."

"Then?"

"They stayed awhile, then left."

Mary Lou let her scarf fall open and tugged on the edges. The dogs fell back, uncharacteristically subdued. The women stood in the vestibule making no motion to go farther. The air thickened with foreboding. I freed Candy and gave her a warning to stay. Surprisingly, she did.

"Did they say where they were going?" Mary Lou asked.

"They talked about skating with the Ice Spinners. They wanted to make the most of one of their last vacation days."

The two mothers exchanged a look. Jackie said, "They didn't come back with the others, and it's getting late, and..." She trailed off, her voice growing increasingly tremulous. "No one remembered seeing them. We're getting worried."

Judging from their expressions, that was a massive understatement.

"We thought—hoped—they might still be here," Mary Lou said.

"I'm sorry. I wish I could help you."

"Something happened to them," Jackie said. "We'd better call the police. It'll be dark soon, and it's supposed to snow."

Her cell phone blared out a few notes of Copland. She paled as she listened to the caller. "Okay," she said. "No, they're not here either."

"I've never met two more self-reliant young girls," I said. "Surely there's no need to worry."

Their faces showed they didn't believe me. I didn't believe myself. But it was too early to panic. They might be with friends. They lived close to Jonquil Lane on Sagramore Lake Road. Not yet old enough to drive, they walked everywhere they went.

Dear Lord. They couldn't have gone walking on Huron Court? Anything but that.

Don't borrow trouble, I told myself.

"I'm calling nine-one-one," Mary Lou said.

I felt adrift, feeling the first touches of fear but determined to be a stabilizing force.

"Won't you sit down?" I asked. "I'll make tea. Everything's better with tea, and I have cookies."

Snowflake cookies, made by Jackie's cookie press. A gift from the girls for New Year's Eve. I shouldn't have mentioned them.

"You're kind, Jennet, but we'll be better off at home," Mary Lou said. "And maybe we'll find them there waiting for us," she added. But her voice lacked conviction.

"I just hope that blizzard holds off," Jackie said.

"If I can do anything to help..."

"We'll be in touch," Mary Lou said.

Thirty-seven

All the light seemed to drain out of the day. Literally and figuratively. One minute I'd been gazing at a threat from another world. In the next, a real threat confronted me. Confronted my young friends, that is.

Jennifer and Molly had to be okay. People don't just vanish into the thin air.

My know-it-all inner voice chimed in. *Oh, but they do. This is Foxglove Corners.*

I tried to escape to Phyllis Whitney's *Thunder Heights*, but images of the missing girls paraded through my head. I could see them clearly. On a hot summer day at their lemonade stand. Racing along the beach with the collie Ginger. I could never remember which girl actually owned Ginger as they had always shared her.

Their excitement when they learned about the walk-on parts in Lucy's movie, *Devilwish*. They wanted to be amateur sleuths and collie rescuers like me. Only last fall, they'd spotted Velvet running free at the Apple Fair and enlisted my aid to catch her.

Generally, the country was a safe place for young people. My initial thought, that they had probably visited a friend, was most likely accurate.

Without letting their parents know?

That wasn't like them.

I let the 'friend' theory go. Predators existed in every town. They walked on two legs and four. They drove by offering enticements and sprang out of the woods, driven by hunger. I thought I heard a faint echo of the deep radio-announcer voice that had forecast snow and danger.

Was anybody safe in today's violent world?

I closed my book and fussed with my table, set the baked ham in the refrigerator, reread the day's weather on my cell phone, and gazed mindlessly out the window. I simply couldn't settle on one activity.

Where were they?

~ * ~

I wasn't sure when the idea to conduct a private search of the roads and by-roads of Foxglove Corners occurred to me. The blizzard was hours away, and everything was ready for my New Year's Eve party with Crane. The police were capable and dedicated, but they couldn't be everywhere.

Common sense tried to intervene. It might well be a futile endeavor. But I'd focus on the area around Sagramore Lake Road, the girls' home. Maybe I'd summon my courage and drive down Huron Court.

And maybe not. Surely they wouldn't venture onto that accursed road, having heard of its grim proclivities.

Ideally, I should have a companion, but who? Leonora had recovered from her Christmas sick spell and gone to a ski resort with Jake. Julia, Annica, and Lucy were...Where? Probably not at the Hunt Club Inn as it was still early. I didn't want to intrude on their festive mood.

Brent? I had to leave a message on his voice mail. He was probably at the Inn making last minute arrangements for his party. It was New Year's Eve, I reminded myself. People were busy. That left the canine contingent. My eyes came to rest on Misty, my incredible psychic collie. She was watching me more closely than the other dogs.

I sent Crane a text telling him of my plan, found my warmest down coat, and attached Misty's leash to her collar.

"I'll be back soon," I told the anxious collies as I led Misty through the door.

"Watch the house."

As I drove out to the lane, I glanced at the section of roadway where Margaret had tried in vain to see the mysterious green house obscured by time's snow fog, while the sleigh stood still and the horses stamped their desire to move on. All ghosts.

In the back, Misty pressed her nose against the window, taking in the passing scenery. She loved to go on car rides, and I loved having a collie companion, one who matched my mood whatever it was.

But no familiar figures appeared in the unrelenting white winter world.

I pressed the button that turned on the CD player Crane had installed in the Focus, and the car filled with a happy melody: *Giddy up jingle horse, pick up your feet...*

A snowflake landed on the windshield, then several. When the melodious notes of my cell phone rang out, I pulled to the side of the road. Once again, I saw Grace's name and number.

"Are you all right?" I asked.

"Sort of. This is my day for seeing things. There's a collie running free in the road. Lily went out to try to coax her inside, but she ran into the woods."

"Did you see a stray or a ghost?"

"A ghost, I'm pretty sure. She wore a red collar. I could hear it jingling from inside the house."

"That sounds like Nana."

"I think so, yes. I have a feeling that the sleigh is near. Perhaps it's circling my house even as we speak."

"It may be," I said.

"Could you drive out this way? I'm excited but a bit uneasy. What if they come for me? I know I said I didn't mind dying, but I find that I do."

"I'm not far from your house now." I told her about Jennifer and Molly and my idea to cruise up and down the wintry roads looking for them.

"That's terrible," Grace said. "This is no time to go missing. I'll keep my eyes peeled for them."

Which meant she'd watch the road from the safety of her palatial mansion.

"I'll stop by, but just for a minute," I said and pulled back to the road.

More snowflakes fell. I turned on the windshield wiper. The unplowed pavement was starting to feel slippery, and I began to rethink my impulsive decision.

Jennet, you're tempting fate. Go home and hope you arrive in one piece. Let the police brave the roads.

But by now, I was approaching the Frost Lake Estates. I'd go a little further, only up to the lake, stop briefly at Grace's house, then go home.

That was my plan.

~ * ~

Frost Lake.

Grace had captured the spirit of Frost Lake as well as its ambience in the small painting she had given me. Islands of snow and chunks of jagged ice lay lightly on its smooth surface. I could tell it was completely frozen over.

Dark woods formed a glowering background for the lake, accentuating the isolation of this particular part of Foxglove Corners. I'd passed the last house ten minutes ago.

In the backseat, Misty gave a short inquisitive yelp. She had been so quiet until now I'd almost forgotten her. I turned to stroke her head and gazed out at the lake, entranced.

In the next instant, a blur of golden fur stepped out of the woods and padded to the lake's edge. The blur took on the shape of a collie. It looked like Brent's Nova, but it couldn't be. He would never let her out of his sight. It could only be the ghost dog, Nana.

I left the engine running and took Misty out onto what would be the lake's beach in the summer. My boots sank down into a deep drift. The dog, no doubt the one Grace had seen, stood like a golden ice sculpture across the frozen lake, her eyes trained on me.

"Nana!" I called.

At the sound of my voice, she turned tail and ran back into the woods.

Wouldn't a ghost have just vanished?

Misty gave a mighty tug on the leash and stepped out onto the lake. Panicking, I yanked hard and brought her back to my side. The ice had cracked at the lake's rim and possibly in other places as well. All I'd need was to have Misty fall into a hole and be unable to scramble back out. She was too heavy for me to lift.

There was no sign of the golden dog. Just to make certain, I swept the area carefully with my eyes. No sign but...A black mitten had gotten caught in the branches of a scraggly bush. Misty had already discovered it and was trying to tug it loose.

With a start, I realized I'd seen it before, or one like it. Jennifer had worn similar mittens with a matching scarf. I'd admired the glitter of the pink and blue thread embedded in the yarn.

I pulled it free from the branch and held it out of Misty's reach. The material was on its way to freezing, but I didn't think it had been here long.

Could the girls have come this far to skate on Frost Lake?

No. I remembered. The Ice Spinners had chosen another lake for their New Year's Eve skating party. One closer to Sagramore Lake Road. Besides, anyone could tell that the ice on Frost Lake was unstable, and no one would come to this isolated, albeit atmospheric, lake to have fun. Especially not on foot.

Misty sniffed the mitten and whined. I was pretty sure she recognized Molly's scent.

Coincidence it might be, but the police had to know. Lieutenant Mac Dalby would make one of his condescending remarks about my interfering with the law, but I had to take the chance.

Had Molly lost her mitten or left it behind as a sign that she had been at Frost Lake? But how strange. A mitten was the last thing one would choose to be without in this icy weather.

Before going back to the car to make my call, I surveyed the area again. If the girls had been at Frost Lake, they'd left the area. Still, I called their names and listened to the echo, so eerie in this beautiful but godforsaken wilderness.

There was of course no answer, but a high, clear sound insinuated itself into the stillness.

Sleigh bells.

Thirty-eight

The sleigh? Now?

Why not? According to Grace, it was in the neighborhood.

The flurries had strengthened into a full-fledged snow squall, and the wind had picked up. I hurried back to the car, dragging a protesting Misty away from the lake. We would wait in a safe, warm place for the phantom sleigh to pass.

The bells were louder now, and Edmund's song wafted through the air:

Now the holly bears the berry as blood it is red,

And Mary bore Jesus who rose from the dead...

He was singing alone.

The sleigh burst out of the snow, Nicholas at the helm. He was heading in my direction! I wasn't in the road, not in his path, but that didn't matter to him. Once again we were on a collision course.

Get away! Clear the path!

No time. No room.

Just do it!

I stamped down hard on the accelerator and steered to the right. Out of the way. With a cry that sounded as if it had originated from a human throat, Misty fell forward off the seat and hit the floor. The car shuddered to a stop, the engine dead.

And Mary bore Jesus, our savior for to be,
And the first tree in the greenwood, it was the holly...

I leaned against the wheel, stunned, my heart pounding. In that moment, I couldn't move, even when I heard Misty crying.

Holly! Holly!

The sleigh thundered past me, using every one of the approximate two feet I'd given it, and plunged into the lake. I watched in horror as it disappeared into its depths. Broken ice exploded into the air and settled back down on the lake's surface.

Gradually, my heartbeat slowed. The ability to think returned.

There should have been noise. Wood breaking apart, flesh tearing. Screaming at least. But silence held the lake in an iron grip. I could hear Misty panting and my own ragged breathing. The bells were gone, the carol ended, although it seemed as if the echo of *'Holly'* lingered over the lake.

I listened. No. Nothing.

Already the shattered ice had reformed itself. The lake looked as it had when I'd first seen it minutes ago. Smooth as glass with isles of ice and snow lying still in the afternoon light.

It made sense. The accident had happened long ago. What I'd seen was a ghostly reenactment. Now, I alone knew what had happened to the riders. Nicholas, weary, lost, blinded by snow, had driven off the road and, all unknowingly, steered the sleigh into Frost Lake—where they still remained, the people, their sleigh, their horses.

Lines from Shakespeare slipped into my mind: *Full fathom five thy father lies. Of his bones are coral made. Those are pearls that were his eyes...*

May they rest in peace, I thought.

The snow had stopped, squall and flurries fled with the wind.

But *were* the lost ones at peace?

Perhaps they would be now that their grave had been discovered, their mystery solved.

So the haunting was over, and I had survived the last encounter with the phantom sleigh.

But was it over?

What about the dog?

~ * ~

As I sat in my car, trying to calm Misty and summon the energy and equilibrium to drive back home in the snow, I remembered Molly and Jennifer and the call I'd been going to make.

We were both shaken to the core, my dog and I. I'd half expected to see the sleigh again, had expected it to vanish in a cloud of snow as usual. I hadn't thought to witness its last hurrah.

They couldn't drag a lake in the winter. They'd have to wait for the ice to melt in spring.

More to the point, would anyone believe what I'd seen and be moved to search for the remains of the sleigh and its occupants?

Certainly Crane would. And Lucy. And Grace. All of us believers.

Certainly Mac wouldn't.

"Rest in peace," I said. "Auralee, Margaret, Edmund, Nicholas. And your faithful horses."

And your dog?

Had I just seen her spirit across the frozen lake staring at me? Shouldn't she be with Auralee?

I felt like crying, but I had to go home and regroup.

First I needed to contact Mac.

~ * ~

Because Mac was a longtime friend of ours, his private cell number was on speed dial. My hand shook as I held my phone; my voice trembled as I relayed my message.

To my surprise, he believed me.

"We've been searching high and low for those kids. We just got a tip."

"You have to search the area around Frost Lake," I told him, turning the mitten over and over in my hand, wondering what tale it could tell. It had thawed, and now, was merely damp. No one would want to put it on.

"I found a mitten. I'm sure it's Molly's."

"We're on our way. You should be home, Jennet," he added. "That's where Crane thinks you are."

"Not if he listened to my message. What kind of tip did you get?" I asked.

He paused. "I'll tell you later. You're at Frost Lake now?"

"Yes."

"I'm guessing you won't go home if I tell you to?"

"You're guessing right. I have to know if the girls are going to be okay."

"Wait there then. Lock the car. See you soon."

He no sooner ended the call than I heard the distant wail of a siren.

What kind of tip could he possibly have received?

Misty had climbed over the seat and sat beside me, her body stone-hard and unyielding, her eyes fastened to me. My velcro collie. She'd been as affected as I had, only in a different way.

The mitten lay in my lap, its blue and pink threads sparkling. It wasn't a minor supernatural phenomenon. It was the yarn.

Approximately ten minutes passed. A patrol car came to a stop in the road, and its siren cut off. Mac strode over the dead vegetation I'd crashed in my frantic attempt to escape the sleigh. I didn't intend to tell him about the sleigh. He'd never believe me.

He speared me with that blue-eyed gaze that suffered no fools and took no prisoners. Misty growled at him.

"Nice collie," he said. "One of yours?"

"Yes. Her name is Misty." I handed him the mitten. "I found this here."

"It fits the description we have of Molly's outerwear," he said. "What are you doing at this remote lake on New Year's Eve? Shouldn't you be at a party or something?"

"I've been looking for the girls. We've been friends for ages. Who gave you a tip?"

"It's more of a confession," he said. "Two teenaged boys from the girls' school admitted they left Molly and Jennifer at the lake as a prank. They went back for them, but by then they had gone."

I gasped. "That's criminal. They could have frozen to death."

That might already have happened. Then these kids would be guilty of murder.

"When they heard the girls were missing, their dads brought them to the station."

"What horrible friends," I said.

"Their names are Dale and Joseph. They belong to some ice-skating club."

I imagined the boys were attractive and, to use an old-fashioned phrase, sweet talkers. Possibly they were older. They'd have to be if they had a car.

A disturbing parallel formed in my mind. Two girls, two handsome, winsome young men. Snow. The lake. Danger.

Could the sleigh have led me to this place so that Molly and Jennifer would be saved, and, in the process, I would learn the truth of the missing sleigh?

On the surface, it seemed incredible. But nothing about this entire affair was believable.

Thirty-nine

Mac stood knee deep in snow, his hand on the front door of the Ford. The flashing lights of his patrol car cast sinister shadows on the ground.

"I repeat, Jennet. It's New Year's Eve. Most people are celebrating."

"You're not."

"I'm on duty."

"Crane and I are spending the evening at home," I said.

"You'd better get there then."

"Not until I know Molly and Jennifer are safe."

He shook his head. "I give up. Crane has his hands full with you."

"Happy New Year," I said.

He looked back once, his face grim.

Good. He was doing his job. I had half a tank of gas and a good heater. I could wait.

Another patrol car pulled up and, in its wake, an ambulance. I opened my purse, hoping to find a snack, and pulled out a Hershey bar. Misty observed me, desire plain in her gaze.

I broke off a square and realized how hungry I was. "Chocolate is bad for dogs," I reminded her.

But if we were here much longer, I'd break into my emergency stash in the trunk and give her a biscuit.

I gazed across the lake. What had the girls done when they realized that Dale and Joseph weren't coming back? Where would they go?

Not into the woods, I hoped, thinking of coyotes and other predators, not to mention a perilous trek across a frozen body of water. They could have started walking. To where?

I noted lights moving into the close-growing trees beyond the lake. The searchers would have approached the woods from another road. Mac hadn't come alone.

All I could do was wait and pray that help hadn't come too late. I picked up the mitten and let it lie on my lap. Why had Molly taken it off?

~ * ~

About an hour later, the rescue team brought the two girls out of the woods and whisked them away in the ambulance. I didn't have a chance to talk to them. Fortunately, Mac was generous with his information.

"They should be all right. One of the girls, Molly, has a sprained ankle. She says she slipped on the ice. They're dehydrated and hungry. Scared more than anything. They were afraid they wouldn't be found."

"They're taking them to the hospital?"

He nodded. "For observation."

"Where were they?" I asked.

"Luckily, they found an abandoned hunter's shack, unheated, of course, and they didn't have any way of calling for help. Their purses with their cell phones were in Dale's car."

"So were they just going to stay in the shack? Who would even know it was there?"

"Just overnight," Mac said. "They planned to hike out to the road in the morning and hope to catch a ride back home."

"With Molly's sprained ankle?"

"They were going to make the attempt."

"There's hardly any traffic in the area," I pointed out.

"Precisely."

"They're lucky to be alive. Those boys should be made to pay for that stupid so-called prank."

"They will," Mac said.

I wished he'd been more specific. Those boys deserved a real punishment, not the proverbial slap on the wrist.

Molly and Jennifer had been left without phones or food or even water. And did the pranksters know that Molly had suffered a sprained ankle?

At least they were alive and safe. I hoped that in the future they would choose their friends more carefully. In their defense, however, how could they have anticipated the hazardous turn their winter outing would take?

"You can leave anytime, Jennet," Mac said. "It'll be dark before long. I want you safe home by then."

"I'm leaving now," I said.

I glanced at Misty who had been eying Mac with suspicion.

"You should get that dog in a crate," he added.

I nodded. No use arguing when he was right.

Home sounded wonderful to me. Crane and I would most likely arrive at the same time, and my New Year's Eve dinner was waiting for us: ham ready to be warmed and served, champagne, a lemon meringue pie, and silver paper bells glittering in the lights of the chandelier. All of our other dogs, the faithful guardians of our house, would gather around us.

"Ready, Misty?" I asked.

She woofed and pressed her nose against the glass as I drove away from Frost Lake, bidding a silent farewell to the lost ones who rested beneath the ice.

~ * ~

After dinner, we sat in the living room waiting for midnight. As the flames leapt and danced in the fireplace, the scents of applewood mixed with balsam wafting through the warm air. Candlelight shone on Crane's hair, turning it to silver. I leaned against his shoulder, safe and warm and happy.

Misty and Halley slept close together in front of the fireplace. From time to time, Misty uttered a soft whimper, perhaps dreaming of the sleigh that fell through the ice.

The storm had arrived. The splattering of moisture on the windows sounded like sleet. It was supposed to turn to snow after midnight.

Thanks heavens we were already home and wouldn't have to navigate icy roads. I spared a thought for Julia and my friends at the Hunt Club Inn, along with Molly and Jennifer in the hospital. All safe for now. If necessary, Julia, Annica, and Lucy could spend the night at the Inn. Or Brent could take them home. He didn't mind driving in treacherous weather.

Crane refilled our flutes with champagne. "I guess you've seen the last of the phantom sleigh."

"I assume so, now that they showed me what happened to them. I wish I could be sure, though, but they they'd have to drag the lake."

"It's frozen solid."

"I saw some cracks in the ice at the lake's edge. I had to hold tight to Misty's leash. She wanted to go exploring."

"No wonder no one ever found them," Crane said. "How could Nicholas have driven the sleigh into the lake? Couldn't he see it?"

"Not with all the snow." I pulled up a memory from long ago, one I had happily buried.

"One time, I was driving at night in the snow. I thought I was staying on the road, but at one point, I realized that I'd veered onto someone's property. A house was being built, so nobody lived there. It was getting harder and harder to drive through the snow. Then my car stopped when I hit a snowdrift. I was about four feet away from a pond. I could have driven right into it."

"Someone was looking out for you."

"My guardian angel," I said. "A passerby saw what had happened and freed my car from the drift. It started, and I drove back to the road. End of story."

I had been so lucky. In danger many times, someone or something had always come to my rescue.

"I've been thinking about the purpose of the apparition," I said. "I think it was to lead me to Molly and Jennifer. I knew they were near when Misty found the mitten."

There were holes in my theory, among them the other times I'd seen the sleigh, long before I knew that Molly and Jennifer were in trouble.

"Didn't you say the boys had an attack of remorse and went to the station?" Crane asked.

"Yes. When they learned the police were searching for two missing girls. They knew they'd be busted."

"So they would have been saved anyway."

I tapped him gently on the arm. "Don't ruin a good ghost story, Crane."

I took a sip of champagne and glanced at the tree and the sleigh ornament shining beneath a frosty white light. Goodbye to my Christmas mystery. Except...

A memory stirred. The dog I'd seen across Frost Lake. The one I'd thought for an instant was Nova until she vanished, and I knew she was Nana, the ghost dog who ran with the sleigh.

Had she perished with the rest? If she walked the woods, did that mean the sleigh riders could also come up out of the lake in spirit form?

Or had Nana never gone down with them but perished in another way?

Unaware of my musings, Crane said, "It's a wrap then. Send the old mysteries out with the old year."

"Not quite," I said. "There's still Brent's problem. We don't know why that woman wants Nova back, or why she accused him of sexual harassment."

"It's her word against his," Crane said, "and, obviously, she has some secret agenda that involves the dog."

"So—now we have a New Year's mystery."

He touched my shoulder. "It never ends, does it?"

"Life is never dull in Foxglove Corners," I said.

The clock began to chime. Three times, six, ten..." Misty raised her head. Seeing all was well, she closed her eyes again.

As the stroke of twelve, Crane pulled me into his arms for a traditional beginning-of-the-new-year kiss that quickly went beyond traditional. "Happy New Year, honey. It was a very good year."

"And next year will be better," I said.

Forty

The sun woke me, throwing dazzling light on the snow-tipped branches visible from the bedroom window. I had slept deeply and without dreaming, all the drama and worry having finally caught up to me.

I was alone. Even our guardian collies of the doorway had deserted me. The door to the guest room was open. Julia must have stayed at the inn last night.

Glancing at the alarm, I saw that it was an incredible eight o'clock. The first day of the new year, and I had wasted two hours of it. A tempting medley of smells drifted up from the kitchen, together with men's voices. Crane was talking to somebody. Brent? Good grief, it was too early for company.

No time to dress. I slipped into my new red velvet robe, my Christmas present from Julia, and ran my fingers through my hair. Wagging her tail, Misty materialized in the hall and escorted me downstairs. As I entered the kitchen, Brent raised his coffee mug in a makeshift salute. "Happy New Year, Jennet."

"Did you sleep well, honey?" Crane asked.

"Too well," I said. "I wanted to make you a special breakfast."

Brent took a sip of his coffee. "You're spoiled, Sheriff. I'm jealous."

Crane indicated a platter of bacon and a large bowl filled with pancake batter. "Got it covered."

I looked out the window. The sleet had indeed turned to snow, and a few errant flakes whirled through the air. The landscape was draped in white and glitter under a bright winter sun. Happy first day of the new year!

"You can help me," Brent said. "Nova's gone."

I poured myself a cup of coffee. No one wants to start a new year with bad news. But fate dishes out the good with the bad, unmindful of the calendar. "How did that happen?"

"I left her with Will at the barn last night. He let her out for a few minutes, and she disappeared."

There was that word again. People disappeared from Brandymere Road and from Huron Court. The girls disappeared while on an ice-skating excursion. Dogs disappeared. Foxglove Corners was notably careless about holding onto its citizens.

Brent slammed his mug on the table and looked instantly regretful.

"Sorry, Jennet. I'm at sixes and sevens. I need to find Nova."

"Your velcro dog," I murmured. "You don't usually leave her on her own."

"Sure I do. You don't think I take her to restaurants or on dates, do you?"

"My point is she wanted to go with you last night. Will inadvertently gave her the chance to follow you."

"We looked all over for her," Brent said. "She knows the way home."

I took a long sip of coffee, thinking. "Maybe she'll turn up at the barn. Stranger things have happened."

I shooed Crane away from the stove. He laid his hand on Brent's shoulder and sat beside him. "Or maybe that woman, that Ava, took her."

"That's what I'm afraid of. What was she doing? Stalking me? Waiting for me to leave Nova unguarded?"

"I wouldn't put it past her," I said. "She probably suspected you'd be going out for New Year's Eve. We never figured out why she wanted Nova so desperately in the first place."

I glanced at the griddle and decided the pancakes could be left unattended for a few minutes.

"We have to do something, and quickly, before she takes Nova to some place where we'll never find her."

"I'm going to keep looking," Brent said. "Will is doing all the 'lost dog' stuff. Calling shelters, making posters, driving through the county."

There was something he should know.

"This may not be relevant, but I thought I saw Nova at Frost Lake yesterday. But it was Nana. It had to be."

"The sheriff told me all about it," Brent said. "My next stop will be Frost Lake."

I admired Brent's determination but didn't want to send him on a wild goose chase. Make that wild ghost chase.

"Did Nova have a red collar?" I asked.

"I bought new collars for all the dogs for Christmas. Nova's was red."

I frowned. Had I seen Nana or Nova? At the moment, I couldn't remember whether I'd heard jingle bells.

"We'll find her," I told Brent. "Somehow. Come back later. We're having an open house. There's lots of baked ham and other good things."

"I'm not in the mood to celebrate," he said. "But I'll be here. Hopefully with Nova."

~ * ~

My friends came and went during the day, but Brent wasn't one of them. I assumed he hadn't found Nova at Frost Lake, and she hadn't come home. It didn't look good.

Julia was leaving the following morning. I had one more free day before classes resumed at Marston and already had two visits planned. I wanted to see Molly and Jennifer, now discharged from the hospital, and to give Grace more details about the last moments of the phantom sleigh.

"I can hardly believe it," Grace had said when I had called her earlier this morning. "All these years, all the places we looked, and they were so close, practically down the road."

"Down in the lake," I added.

"For some reason, for all its beauty, Frost Lake has never been popular with people," Grace said. "I'd like to have proof," she added.

"We'll have to wait until the spring thaw. You don't have to believe me, Grace. I'm only telling you what I saw."

"Oh, I believe you. Lately, I had a feeling they were near. I hoped I'd see them."

I thought about telling her that I'd seen Nana but decided to wait. Let her deal with this grim new discovery first. Also, I didn't understand why the dog and the sleigh had parted company. I'd been thinking Auralee had gone down to her death with her collie in her arms.

"I'm so glad your young friends are all right," Grace said.

"They will be."

"Stop over tomorrow if you can."

I promised I would, imagining that she would like to hear the story again, hoping I would remember an additional detail or two.

She didn't ask about Nana.

~ * ~

"I'm off to my quiet life up north," Julia said the next morning as she donned her heavy down coat. "Something's always going on in Foxglove Corners. I'm going to miss all the excitement."

I hugged her. "Drive carefully and come back soon. Maybe I can scare up a ghost or two for you."

"Do that," she said. "I'll call when I get home."

Before I had a chance to miss her, I bundled myself up and drove the short distance to Sagramore Lake Road. Both of the girls were at Molly's house, eating popcorn, drinking pop, and reading the series books I'd given them for Christmas. Ginger lay between them, gazing at first one, then the other, hoping for treats from the popcorn bowl.

"I guess I won't be ice skating anymore," Molly said.

"Don't say that," Jennifer told her. "We just had bad luck."

"Slipping on ice, you mean?"

"No, going out with a pair of losers. We should have stayed with the Ice Spinners."

Molly placed a bookmark reverently in the old volume she was reading. "These girls have adventures and get into all kinds of danger, but they get themselves out of it. They don't end up in the hospital."

"That's fiction, Molly," I said. "It's good reading fun, but it isn't life."

"I didn't think I'd like this book, but I really do, even if it doesn't have a collie in it," she said.

"I'm glad. Can you tell me what happened? I know the bare bones of it."

Jennifer looked at Molly. "I'll do it, Molly. These guys...We liked them. All the girls did. They asked us to go skating with them on a new lake. When we got there, we were the first ones out of the car. While Molly was taking a picture of the lake, they just took off. Our purses and lunches, everything, were in that car."

"I couldn't believe they would do that," Molly said. "I don't want to see them again. Ever."

"We'll have to, Molly. We go to the same school."

"They humiliated us," she said. "We don't have to talk to them."

"They humiliated themselves by playing that awful trick on you," I pointed out. "Their friends will never look at them the same way again."

"Our friends will think we were dumb."

"Maybe," I said. "You were trusting, and, to a point, that's a good quality. By the way, I'd like to know how you came to find that shack."

"That's the only good part," Molly said. "The dog led us to it."

Forty-one

"What dog?" I asked.

"The collie," Molly said. "She was just there. It was right after I fell on the ice. I took off my mitten to see if I broke my ankle."

Ah! And that mitten stayed behind on the bush until Misty noticed it.

"It hurt so much," she continued. "I didn't want to move. The dog kept barking at us. Then she ran a little way off, wagged her tail, and came back."

"Like Lassie." Jennifer took up the tale. "We thought she belonged to a house nearby where we could call home, but she led us into the woods."

"I was afraid," Molly admitted. "I didn't want to go. I didn't think I could walk. Jennifer said we should trust the dog. Then we saw this little old house in the woods. The door was unlocked."

"We were so cold," Jennifer added.

For a moment, I heard an echo of Auralee's lament in Jennifer's voice. Auralee shivering as she sat in the sleigh, lost and frightened. *I'm so cold.*

"It was better inside, but not much warmer," Molly said. "There wasn't anything in the house. Not even a chair. But at least we were out of the wind. And I was so thirsty." She took a swig of her root beer. "I've been thirsty ever since."

"Would you like a Coke, Jennet?" Jennifer asked.

On such a cold day? Not really. "I'm good," I said. "What happened to the dog?"

"I don't know," Molly said. "She didn't stay with us. I thought she went for help, but she didn't come back."

She had done her part by leading the girls to shelter. As for nearby houses, there weren't any, but they couldn't know that.

"I have another question," I said. "Did the dog have a red collar with jingle bells on it?"

Molly brightened. "Yes, she did. I forgot. She sounded like one of Santa's reindeer running through the woods."

I had one last question—for myself—but no one to answer it. Had the dog who'd led the girls to the house been Nana or Nova?

~ * ~

Grace said, "When we know for certain that they're at the bottom of Frost Lake, I want to place a memorial there. A cross, maybe, or a stone sleigh with the names of my Aunt Auralee and her friends engraved on it."

"I see a couple of problems with that," I said. "The ground is frozen, and you'll have to get permission from whoever owns the land."

"I can't imagine anyone would object, and I can wait until spring. I talked to Mr. Cameron Lodge at the *Banner*. He's sending a reporter to interview me. He thinks the story will interest his readers."

A silent alarm went off in my mind. "Don't give him my name. I do *not* want everyone to know I saw the sleigh."

"But how else would I know it was at the bottom of Frost Lake?" she asked.

"Think of something. You had an extremely graphic dream. You consulted a psychic. You saw the phantom sleigh yourself. Anything."

"As you wish," she said, "but this talent you have is a wonderful gift. You shouldn't hide it."

"I suppose so. It can also be frightening."

And there were several downsides to publicity. One time, I had almost lost Winter, a dog I'd rescued, because a story about his heroic deed had been printed in the paper. Also, I didn't want my students to know about my so-called talent.

I left soon after. For all her initial elation at finally knowing the truth, Grace had lapsed into a strange mood.

"I'm the only one left who cares that the old mystery is finally solved," she said. "Everyone else is dead. That's what happens when you get old."

I couldn't argue with her, but neither could I take the depressing sentiment to heart.

~ * ~

The best of holidays comes to an inevitable end. Christmas trees and wreaths can last into January, and glitter never seems to go away. But for most people, it's back to life in a new year. A new beginning. For me, it was back to school.

The next day I packed a lunch, brought my schoolbooks out of temporary storage, and picked up Leonora for the long drive to Oakpoint. A dusting of snow covered the road, and I had to dodge about a hundred icy patches, but overall the commute was uneventful.

"Did Brent ever find his collie?" Leonora asked.

"Not as of yesterday. We think that woman who accused him of fondling her took Nova. We still don't know why."

"She had to have a reason."

"If we knew what it was, we'd have a chance to find Nova. I feel I've let Brent down."

"What could you do?" she asked.

"Without any leads, nothing. And time's passing. We may never see Nova again."

I didn't want to accept that. Brent appeared to have exhausted his resources but didn't like to deal with failure. Neither did I.

"She won't be going after Brent now that she got what she wanted," I said.

"That's something."

It was. Ava's accusation was only a means to an end and a horrible one at that.

As soon as we reached Marston, I was forced to put thoughts of Nova aside. The first day after a long recess is never easy, especially with Principal Grimsley calling an unscheduled staff meeting for the following day.

Student attendance was poor. Classes were either rowdy, still in holiday mode, or sleepy. Some students had traveled out of state for the holidays and were late returning to Michigan. Others, undoubtedly, wanted to spend an extra hour in bed. My best laid lesson plans fell by the wayside.

Well, the week was young.

Something strange or, rather, unusual, happened in my English Literature class. One of my students, Vicky, asked me if I'd heard about the new Lassie movie being made for television.

Vicky's inquiry was strange because I never talked about my life away from Marston High School with my classes. But there was that poster of a collie puppy in the snow on my bulletin board...

"I know you like collies," Vicky said.

"Will it be a remake of *Lassie Come Home*?" I asked.

"It takes place in the future after wars and bombs destroy most of the cities. Lassie and her family are trying to survive."

"Well, that *is* different," I said. "Do you know what the movie is called?

All she knew was that the title had Lassie's name in it.

"I'll see what I can find out about it," I said, although it didn't sound like anything I'd want to see.

Eventually, the last bell rang, and I found myself back in Foxglove Corners, with Leonora dropped off and the comfort of home a mere fifteen minutes away.

Just in time. Snowflakes went swirling through the air, blown by a gusty wind. I turned on the windshield wipers and lights and followed the road as it curved through a stretch of gloomy woodland. As I passed a small lake half-hidden by a stand of pine, I heard sleigh bells ringing.

No! Not again! The haunting was supposed to be over. The sleigh had reached the end of its last ride, leaving driver and passengers beneath the ice of Frost Lake.

You're hearing the bells of one of Fred Farmer's sleighs-for-hire.

The bells were loud and clear, but I couldn't tell whether they were behind or in front of me. I pulled to the side of the road, took deep breaths and waited, willing my heartbeat to slow down.

Sleigh-for-hire... Sleigh-for-hire...

Their diabolical clanging of the bells grew louder every minute. There was nothing merry about them. On the contrary, they were discordant. Unnatural. Bells that originated in another world.

The sleigh sailed into view, the horses clip clopping on the gravel, and came to a sudden stop. The horses were like animals on a merry-go-round, stalled in mid-trot by a power failure, along with the sleigh they were supposed to be pulling.

Time stood still.

And the people, the ghosts...I saw them clearly and heard their voices, somehow audible above the shrieking of the bells.

"What fun!" Auralee cried. "Can't you go faster, Nicholas?"

"Slow is better. Enjoy the scenery."

"Let's have a song," Edward said.

Margaret brushed snow from the cover of her songbook. "Yes, a Christmas song. Which one shall it be?"

Nicholas took his eyes off the road ahead for an instant. "How about Jingle Bells? We're dashing through the snow." He started singing.

Auralee pulled her silver necklace out from the folds of her coat and held it.

As if it were a talisman.

Like the bells, the singing was unnaturally loud.

Now the ground is white,
Go it while you're young,
Take the girls tonight,
And sing this sleighing song.

I was seeing the apparition at the beginning of the sleigh's journey, begun when the world was younger and more innocent and every inch of it sparkled with a generous scattering of diamond dust.

An odd thought came to me. If I were to steer the car into the sleigh, would I drive through it? Should I try it? The sleigh, while it appeared solid enough, couldn't possibly be substantial.

Could it?

Setting aside what I knew, it looked real. That was what mattered. I would never have the nerve to drive into it.

So I watched and listened. Presently the wind blew a high wave of snow over the sleigh, and it vanished. The singing and ringing blew into the wind and died.

I couldn't follow it now. Surely, the sleigh didn't intend for me to follow it to Frost Lake a second time.

Go *home*, I told myself. *Build a fire. Drink a cup of tea. Play with the dogs. Wait for Crane. It's a new year.*

I pulled back out to the road.

A sable and white collie stepped daintily out of the woods, stood in my path, and stared at me.

A Lassie dog.

The dog who ran with the sleigh.

Forty-two

The collie wore a red collar. As she came closer, the jingle bells attached to it rang. The sound was crisp and clear and melodious, not at all like the ghostly sleigh bells that had recently assaulted my ears.

Again, I pulled to the side of the road. Leaving the engine running, I approached the dog.

"Nana?"

I waited for her to vanish in a puff of snow. It didn't happen.

Wagging her tail, she bounded up to me and circled around me barking joyfully, her dark eyes gleaming.

She knew me. She was Nova.

The fur on her legs, once snowy white, was begrimed with dirt, and burrs and noxious seeds were stuck to her coat.

"Nova, come," I said.

She needed no further enticement. I opened the door, and she jumped into the driver's seat. My seat.

I stroked her and ruffled her fur, my hand making contact with all sorts of forest matter she'd picked up in the wood.

"I'm so happy, *so* happy, to see you."

She nudged my hand playfully and tugged at my gloves.

"I love you, too," I said. "But move over, out of my seat. You're going home."

At this hour, Brent would be at the barn. As I altered my homeward-bound course, I carried on a one-sided conversation with Nova.

"Everyone has been looking for you. Brent misses you. He's going to be so happy to see you."

Ears alert, she seemed to understand me. At least she was listening.

"Tell me what happened to you," I said.

She tilted her head.

If only she could. How often I'd lamented the fact that dogs couldn't talk.

"Did you run away from home?" I asked. "Did that horrible woman take you?"

Would we ever know?

I let the thought of hot tea by the fire fade away. It seemed as if I was doomed to drive on snowy roads forever with darkness fast approaching. But happiness at bringing joy to another shortened the drive. Before long, I reached Brent's barn. He was carrying cartons out of his vintage Plymouth.

I hurried out of the car, stepping deep in snow. "I brought you a belated Christmas present."

He had already seen Nova, and she had seen him.

"Nova! Is it really Nova?"

She pawed at the window, ears flattened, barking loudly. It was hard to tell whether master or dog was more excited.

Brent opened the door, and she jumped at him, almost unbalancing him. One of the cartons fell to the ground.

"How did you find her, Jennet?"

"I followed the sleigh," I said. "It was magical."

I tried to ignore the icy shiver that stole over my body.

Had the sleigh led me to Nova?

Preposterous. Coincidence. Why would the apparition care about uniting a dog with its owner? Its mission was to show me how the sleigh riders had met their end.

Will came out of the barn and stopped in his tracks. "Nova?"

Nova left Brent's side and danced around Will's boots, offering Will her paw to shake. *Was it the wind making my eyes water? I didn't think so.*

"You need a bath, girl," Will said.

"And food, I'll bet," I said.

Brent handed the cartons to Will and picked up the one that had fallen on the ground. "She can have some of my roast beef with her dinner," he said.

"And my carrots. She loves carrots. There are carrots with the beef, aren't there?"

"Sure, and potatoes."

The talk reminded me of a hungry husband on his way home and no doubt expecting dinner on the stove.

"I love being part of this this reunion, but it's getting late," I said. "I have to get home."

Along with creating a dinner from scratch, I needed some quiet time to think. I hoped I could make it home without hearing sleigh bells.

~ * ~

Home at last. I took steaks out of the freezer and supervised a snow-play session with the dogs. They were in a frenzy. As soon as I'd taken off my parka, they'd fallen on it, sniffing intently. Nova's scent puzzled them. I could imagine the thoughts spinning around in their minds.

Another dog? Where is she?

Inspired by Vicky's comments in class, an idea had been forming in the back of my mind. Now it nagged at me. With preparations for dinner taken care of, I turned on my computer and searched for 'Lassie,' 'Movies about Lassie' and whatever else I could think of.

In the end, it was ridiculously easy to find what I was searching for. In fact, in the week before Christmas the *Banner* had carried the story of the planned mini- series, *Lassie: The Last Dog on Earth*, as well as a follow-up article that made every mysterious happening clear.

The movie's canine star, a collie named Nova, owned and trained by breeder Ralph Carstairs, had gone missing, presumably stolen from Carstairs' kennel. He and the producer offered a reward of five thousand dollars for her return.

How was it possible that none of us had noticed the article?

Well, the holidays had been a busy time. I'd seen it now and could figure out what must have happened.

For some reason, perhaps anticipating a reward, Ava had stolen Nova from Carstairs. Presumably, the very determined Nova had run away from Ava and ended up in the shelter, having been rescued from the road by a passing Good Samaritan. Ava had extracted Brent's contact information from the volunteer at the shelter.

Her story—a child stricken with cancer, his dog given away—and her outrageous accusation of Brent had been fabrications, her intent obviously to retrieve Nova and collect the reward money. Once again, she had stolen Nova, this time from Brent's barn, and once again, Nova had escaped from her clutches.

Over the top, I thought. But in my mind, it all came together. To be sure, I was filling in blanks without solid evidence, but I didn't care. Nova was back with Brent who loved and wanted her. All's well that ends well. Except...

Oh darn. It wasn't, not really. Nova belonged to a man named Ralph Carstairs, and he wanted her back.

Forty-three

"I wish I'd never read that story about Nova," I said to Crane that evening. "I suppose I should tell Brent."

I gazed at the flames in the fireplace and waited, hoping Crane would say that some secrets should be kept or that I should leave well enough alone. Of course, he didn't.

"Brent would want to know, Jennet," he said. "And the truth may come out anytime."

"He adopted Nova from a legitimate shelter," I said. "That should count for something. Now they're bonded. They were so happy to be reunited."

"There's a chance that Nova isn't Carstairs' dog."

So slim a chance it might break apart at any moment.

"I never believed that story Ava and her husband concocted," I said.

A child stricken with cancer, his dog given away—it was a tale cleverly designed to tug at somebody's heart strings. But I had seen through it.

"She sure went to a lot of trouble to get her hands on that dog," Crane said.

"For five thousand dollars," I added. "I'll have to tell Brent."

"You will."

I sighed and looked away from the fireplace. The fire provided warmth and atmosphere but no enlightenment. "If only I hadn't seen that sleigh today. Then I wouldn't have seen Nova."

But that wouldn't have been good. I'd wanted to find Nova. We all did.

"I don't understand why you're still seeing the sleigh," Crane said. "I thought that particular haunting was over."

"It appears whenever it snows. What I don't understand is the sleigh's timing. I saw it fall through the ice at Frost Lake and all the riders with it. Now I see them hours earlier—in their time—happy and singing, obviously at the beginning of their ride. It's like they're doomed to relive that experience over and over again. And I'm doomed to see them."

I would have to consult Lucy again. "I wonder if that eternal ride is punishment for something they did."

"Something all four of them did? I doubt it." Crane pulled me close and held me. "Don't worry, Jennet. If you're right about the sleigh coming with the snow, you won't see it in the spring."

"Is that supposed to comfort me? It's only January. We'll have lots of snow in the next two months. I wish I knew how to end this once and for all."

"And I wish I could make it go away for you," he said.

Two wishes that wouldn't likely be granted.

"I don't know what more they want," I said. "The mystery of their disappearance is solved. Grace is determined to have the lake dragged when the ice melts. She's talking about a memorial on the site, but she would like to have proof they're in the lake."

"They may want a proper burial in a cemetery. With a priest and prayers."

"I'm sure Grace will see to that. In the spring."

After the snows of January and February and, maybe, March melt.

The phantom sleigh was my problem, but I couldn't do anything about it at present. If I wanted a restful night, though, there was something else I had to take care of.

"I'd better call Brent," I said, "before I talk myself out of it."

~ * ~

I had braced myself for any number of explosive reactions from Brent when he heard my news, but all he said was, "Are you sure?" His tone was calm but deadly.

"You can read the articles online for yourself. There's no doubt in my mind that Nova is Carstairs' dog."

"I can believe that. She's so clever, even more so than most collies."

"She was trained to be a canine star," I said.

"*My* star."

"Yes, she's yours. Unfortunately, I don't know how a judge would rule."

"Believe me," he said, "it won't come to that. Do you have an address for Carstairs?"

"His kennel is somewhere in Ohio. You can find it online. It's Carstairs Collies, I think."

There was a pause, unusual in a conversation with Brent. "What are you going to do?" I asked.

"I don't know yet, but I'll handle it. Thanks for the heads-up."

I explained my theory about Ava and the reward. "She must have guessed that Carstairs would offer a reward for Nova's return," I said. "She'd know about the movie, or maybe she makes a habit of stealing valuable dogs for reward money."

"She's evil, all right, but she dropped out of sight, and her charges went with her," Brent said. "I have my lawyer on it. I say, 'Good riddance'."

"She shouldn't get off scot free. She stole a dog. She tried to run a scam. She made a false accusation. I wonder if she'll make an attempt to take Nova again."

"Over my dead body," Brent said.

"Let me know what happens," I said. "And keep Nova on a very short leash."

~ * ~

The next day after school, Leonora and I stopped at Dark Gables to visit Lucy. Over tea and cookies, I said, "How can I make this apparition go away?"

"I wish I could help you, Jennet."

How disappointing. "You can't?"

"I don't have any magic tricks up my sleeve. For what it's worth, I think Crane is right. Your ghosts want to have a proper burial in a cemetery."

"For their bones," I murmured.

"Yes, their skeletons. Then their spirits may rest in peace."

"How did this become my responsibility?" I asked.

Lucy shrugged. "You're super-sensitive to the denizens of the world beyond. You came to live in Foxglove Corners where borders between the natural and supernatural are hazy at best."

"I wouldn't have had it any other way," I said, thinking of all the blessings that had come my way since I'd moved to Foxglove Corners. "I'm going to go back to Frost Lake one day soon. Who knows? I might find closure."

"Is that wise?" Lucy asked.

At the same time, Leonora said, "Jennet, no! It's too dangerous."

"What can happen...that hasn't happened already?"

"Anything," Leonora said. "That lake is wicked."

"Nonsense," Lucy countered. "It's just a body of water. If someone drowns in an ocean, you don't blame the ocean."

"I don't want you to risk it," Leonora added. "Then I'd have to drive to school all alone. I'd hate that."

"So would I."

I handed my teacup to Lucy for reading. "What do you see? Something good, please."

She took one brief look at the patterns. "I see a tall, handsome man and a heart. He's blond, not dark, but I'm sure that doesn't matter to you." She brought the cup close to me and pointed to a lopsided valentine.

Crane. Love.

"There's no lake monster waiting to pull her under?" Leonora asked.

Lucy smiled. "There's no danger of that. Besides, the lake has turned to ice."

I chose to believe Lucy. As soon as I could carve a free hour out of my schedule, I intended to drive out to Frost Lake.

And do what?

Just be there and wait for whatever would happen.

Forty-four

Days passed. I didn't hear from Brent. Every night I cooked enough dinner for three, anticipating one of his unannounced visits, and every day it snowed, sometimes only an inch or two, other times flurries.

I postponed my solitary trip to Frost Lake. Grace called frequently, asking if I'd seen the sleigh again. I hadn't. I imagined she didn't completely believe my story about seeing it fall through the ice.

Why not? It made sense, especially since the wreckage of the sleigh had never been found on land. I wondered why nobody had ever thought about the lakes.

At Marston, my classes settled down. January was a crucial month in the school year, a time for winding up courses and preparing for final exams. Then we would all look forward to a new semester and different classes. As always, I had high hopes for fewer rowdy groups.

In my rare free moments, I wondered about Ava. Had she finally given up her scam? Crane thought she might have left town. Having failed to return Nova and secure Carstairs' reward, that was likely. But I would be happier if I had proof that Ava was out of Nova's life for good.

Of course, if Carstairs had regained possession of Nova, he would make certain Ava wouldn't have a chance to snatch her again. That wouldn't be a happy resolution to Nova's story.

I thought of her in the role of the last dog on earth. Would she adapt to the life of a canine actress or long to be with Brent again?

On Sunday afternoon, Brent parked his vintage Plymouth in our driveway and emerged, carrying a large shopping bag emblazoned with the logo of Pluto's Gourmet Pet Shop. Nova padded happily along at his side.

The collies and I went to the door to welcome him, the dogs hungry for the treats they knew he had, as I was hungry for news.

They came in, shedding snow and fur. My dogs flocked around the Pluto's bag. Brent handed it to me.

"You still have her," I said as he freed Nova from the leash. My pack engulfed her with play bows and raucous 'Let's run' barks. "Tell me what happened."

"I persuaded Mr. Carstairs to part with her for an enormous sum. She's worth every penny."

I left the dogs to their rough housing and ushered Brent into the living room. "Make yourself comfortable. I'll get you a cup of coffee."

"And a snack?" he asked.

"I think I can scare one up."

"What happens with the movie?"

"They already replaced Nova with her litter sister, and the show goes on."

"I want to hear everything," I said. "You'll stay to dinner. I have a roast and a banana cream pie."

"My favorites."

Dear, predictable Brent. Whatever I cooked or baked was his favorite.

While we waited for Crane, he told me about his trip to Ohio, and the negotiations with Nova's owner.

"I took her with me," he said. "Carstairs is basically a hard-headed businessman, but he has a sentimental streak. He could see we belong together."

Nova lay at Brent's feet, alongside Misty who hadn't claimed her usual spot on his lap.

"He drove a hard bargain." Abruptly he changed the subject. "We'll have to watch for that movie, sometime this summer."

"It sounds pretty grim to me," I said. "I don't like to think about the end of the world. Even with Lassie in it."

I liked to think I would always live in the green Victorian farmhouse on Jonquil Lane in Foxglove Corners with Crane and our collies. That our lives would never change.

The dogs' barking heralded the arrival of Crane, who would most likely toss a teasing remark Brent's way about visiting me when he wasn't around. Brent would counter with a comment about coming for the food. Then we'd have dinner together while Nova and our dogs played and rested, as dogs will.

The only life I wanted was the one I'd built with Crane in Foxglove Corners.

I couldn't possibly be happier.

~ * ~

On a cold Saturday morning, I left my weekend chores undone and drove to Frost Lake. I'd debated about taking Misty with me, but in the end decided to go alone. I left the engine running and stood near the car, gazing out at the lake and the dark woods behind it.

What did I hope to accomplish? To end the haunting. How could that happen?

Frost Lake was a study in white and silver and a shade of blue so pale it could scarcely be called a color. No snow fell, but a hearty wind shifted powdery flakes from drift to drift and onto the ice that held the lake in a mighty grip.

I had dressed warmly, adding two extra layers, but the air was frigid.

Stay out here long enough, not moving, and you'll turn to an ice sculpture, I told myself.

But I knew I had to do this.

"Nicholas, Auralee, Edmund, Margaret," I said softly. "I've come to see you."

The wind gave a mighty sigh and blew snow in my face. I wiped it away.

How still it was. How beautiful...and eerie. A poignant melody, Edmund's song, played through my mind:

Now, the holly bears the berry as white as the milk,

And Mary bore Jesus who was wrapped up in silk...

My imagination slipped into overdrive. I could almost hear ghostly music rising from the ice barrier, stealing across the frozen lake to lose itself in the woods on its northern side.

And Mary bore Jesus, our savior for to be,

And the first tree in the greenwood, it was the holly.

Holly! Holly!

"How can I help you?" I asked, feeling foolish, but there was no one within several miles to hear me.

Silence.

Well, what did you expect?

The remains of the people I'd addressed lay in a watery grave. Their spirits roamed the roads and by-roads of Foxglove Corners, perpetually reliving their last merry sleigh ride, unable to reach their home, unable to rest.

The silence of this haunted place was overwhelming. Grace had said Frost Lake was an unpopular destination. I could see why. To be sure, it was beautiful and private, but something in the air that hovered over the lake issued a vague warning: *Go away while you can. This is a haunted, unwholesome place.*

I didn't listen. Instead, I allowed my imagination free rein. I remembered Lucy saying that if a person drowns in an ocean, you don't blame the ocean. She also claimed that the walls of a house could absorb and hold echoes of traumatic events. Why couldn't the walls of nature do the same?

I walked up to the very edge of the lake and stood looking down at the expanse of ice, wishing for X-ray vision.

On second thought, did I want to see the elegant sleigh turned to waterlogged pieces of wood? Or see skeletons?

"I'll make a bargain with you," I said. "You can continue your ride through Foxglove Corners, but please, please, don't show yourselves to me again. In exchange, I'll see that your story is known throughout Foxglove Corners and beyond. Grace is going to give you the burial you should have had. If she can't do it for some reason, I will. Okay?"

More silence. But did I hear whispers? Or was it the wind?

The wind. Don't get carried away.

"I'm leaving now," I said.

I stepped back and trod on something hard. At my feet a small object glittered in the sun. It lay on top of the snow like a fallen star. It looked like charm that had broken loose from its chain or bracelet. Perhaps Jennifer or Molly had lost it.

I picked it up. It was a tarnished silver locket.

The locket Auralee had held in the apparition?

Taking off my gloves, I opened it gently with stiffening fingers. The image of a handsome young man with wavy black hair, rugged features, and a rouguish half-mocking smile gazed back at me.

Nicholas? Or Edmund?

No, it must be Nicholas. Auralee had a crush on Nicholas. When it became clear he had lost his way, she had held onto the locket, and no doubt lost it when the sleigh plunged through the ice.

Grace would recognize Auralee's locket. She had known Nicholas.

But why, if it had been lying here on the sand and snow in all the many years that had passed since the accident had no one found it?

I had no answer, but did it matter? In my hand, I held the proof Grace hoped for. When the ice melted, we would find what was left of the lost sleigh. In the meantime, Grace would be overjoyed to have the locket.

I started as a sharp cracking sound broke the stillness, then looked around. Nothing alarming intruded on my solitary visit. Maybe a forest creature had stepped on and broken a branch.

A delicate jingling as fragile as a fairy sound danced on the air. A sable collie with golden fur and a red collar stood on the ice in the middle of the lake watching me with a tilted head.

The dog who ran with the sleigh.

I thought I heard a whine.

Then the wind blew a high wave of snow over the lake, and she was gone.

A moment later, holding the locket safe in my clasped hand, I trudged through the snow back to the car. Back home.

Meet Dorothy Bodoin

Dorothy Bodoin lives in Royal Oak, Michigan, with her blue merle collie, Layla. A graduate of Oakland University with Bachelor's and Master's degrees in English, Dorothy worked as a secretary for Chrysler Missile Corporation, two years of which were spent in southern Italy. For several more years she taught English in a Michigan high school until leaving education to write full-time. She is the author of the Foxglove Corners Mystery Series, six novels of romantic suspense and one Gothic novel. At present, she is working on a Foxglove Corners mystery titled *In the Greenwood He Was Slain.*

Other Works From The Pen Of Dorothy Bodoin

Treasure at Trail's End (Gothic romance) - The House at Trail's End seemed to beckon to Mara Marsden, promising the happy future she longed for. But could she discover its secret without forfeiting her life?

Ghost across the Water (romantic suspense) - Water falling from an invisible force and a ghostly man who appears across Spearmint Lake draw Joanna Larne into a haunting twenty-year-old mystery.

Darkness at Foxglove Corners - Foxglove Corners offers tornado survivor Jennet Greenway country peace and romance, but the secret of the yellow Victorian house across the lane holds a threat to her new life. (#1)

Winter's Tale - On her first winter in Foxglove Corners Jennet Greenway battles dognappers, investigates the murder of the town's beloved veterinarian, and tries to outwit a dangerous enemy. (#3)

A Shortcut through the Shadows - Jennet Greenway's search for the missing owner of her rescue collie, Winter, sets her on a collision course with an unknown killer. (#4)

Cry for the Fox - In Foxglove Corners, the fox runs from the hunters, the animal activists target the Hunt Club, and a killer stalks human prey on the fox trail. (#2)

The Witches of Foxglove Corners - With a haunting in the library, a demented prankster who invades her home, and a murder in Foxglove Corners, Halloween turns deadly for Jennet Greenway. (#5)

The Snow Dogs of Lost Lake - A ghostly white collie and a lost locket lead Jennet Greenway to a body in the woods and a dangerous new mystery. (#6)

The Collie Connection - As Jennet Greenway's wedding to Crane Ferguson approaches, her happiness is shattered when a Good Samaritan deed leaves her without her beloved black collie, Halley, and ultimately in grave danger. (#7)

A Time of Storms - When a stranger threatens her collie and she hears a cry for help in a vacant house, Jennet Ferguson suspects that her first summer as a wife may be tumultuous. (#8)

The Dog from the Sky - Jennet's life takes a dangerous turn when she rescues an abused collie. Soon afterward, a girl vanishes without a trace. Ironically, she had also rescued an abused collie. Is there a connection between the two incidents? (#9)

Spirit of the Season - Mystery mixes with holiday cheer, as a phantom ice skater returns to the lake where she died, and a collie is accused of plotting her owner's fatal accident. (#10)

Another Part of the Forest - Danger rides the air when a kidnapper whisks his victims away in a hot air balloon, and a false friend puts a curses on a collie breeder's first litter. (#11)

Where Have All the Dogs Gone? - An animal activist frees the shelter dogs in and around Foxglove Corners to save them from being destroyed. Running wild in the countryside, they face an equally distressing fate and post a risk to those who come in contact with them. (#12)

The Secret Room of Eidt House - A rabid dog that should have died months ago from the dread disease runs free in the woods of

Foxglove Corners, and the library's long-kept secret unleashes a series of other strange events. (#13)

Follow a Shadow - A shadowy intruder haunts Jennet's woods by night, and a woman who can't accept the death of her collie asks Jennet to help her find Rainbow Bridge where she believes her dog waits for her. (#14)

The Snow Queen's Collie - A white collie puppy appears on the porch of the Ferguson farmhouse during a Christmas Eve snowstorm. In another part of Foxglove Corners a collie breeder's show prospect disappears. Meanwhile, the painting Jennet's sister gave her for Christmas begins to exhibit strange qualities. (#15)

The Door in the Fog - A wounded dog disappears in the fog. A blue door on the side of a barn vanishes. Strange wildflowers and a sound of weeping haunt a meadow. The woods keep their secret, and a curse refuses to die. (#16)

Dreams and Bones - At Brent Fowler's newly purchased Spirit Lamp Inn, a renovation turns up human bones buried in the inn's backyard, rekindling interest in the case of a young woman who disappeared from the inn several decades ago. As Jennet tries to solve this mystery, she doesn't realize it may be her last. (#17)

A Ghost of Gunfire - Months after gunfire erupted in her classroom at Marston High School, leaving one student dead and one seriously wounded, Jennet begins to hear a sound of gunshots inaudible to anyone else. Meanwhile, she resolves to find the demented person who is tying dogs to trees and leaving them to die. (#18)

The Silver Sleigh - Rosalyn Everett was missing and presumed dead. Her collies had been rescued, and her house was abandoned. But a blue merle collie haunts her woods and a figure in bridal white traverses the property. (#19)

The Stone Collie - Jennet's discovery of a collie puppy chained in the yard of a vacant house sets her on a search for a man whose activities may threaten Foxglove Corners' security. Meanwhile, horror story novelist Lucy Hazen is mystified when scenes from her work-in-progress are duplicated in real life. (#20)

The Mists of Huron Court - The house was beautiful, a vintage pink Victorian in a picturesque but lonely country setting, and the girl playing ball with her dog in the yard was friendly, suggesting that she and Jennet walk their dogs together some time. Jennet thinks she has made a new friend until she returns to the house and finds a tumbling down ruin where the Victorian once stood and no sign that the girl and dog have ever been there. ((#21)

Down a Dark Path - What hold does the pink Victorian on Huron Court have on Brent Fowler who is determined to re-create the home of long-dead Violet Randall? When he disappears, could he have been cast adrift in time? (#22))

Shadow of the Ghost Dog - An invisible dog grieves inside the house chosen as a setting for the movie based on Lucy Hazen's book *Devilwish*, and a landscaper unearths a human skeleton in the backyard while planting shrubs. (#23))

The Dark Beyond the Bridge - The discovery of a secret ghost town in a densely rural area of Michigan's lower peninsula leads to mystery and danger for Jennet Ferguson and her friends. (#24)

The Deadly Fields of Autumn - An antique television set that airs an obscure Western at random times and a woman who disappears with her newly-adopted rescue dog draw Jennet into a puzzling mystery. (#25)

The Lost Collies of Silverhedge - Collie breeder Madselin Rivard was dead, leaving her prized, valuable collies uncared for in their kennel. Jennet and her friends rescue five of them, but eight remain unaccounted for. (#26)

All the Pretty Little Collies - Danger stalks the collies of Foxglove Corners when an unknown villain begins tossing poisoned meat into their yards, and a girl with a winning blue merle collie is warned via threatening messages to withdraw her dog from competition or risk the consequences. (#27)

Phantom in the Pond - Brent Fowler's plan to open a house for geriatric collies goes awry when strange things begin to happen in his newly purchased country estate. (#28)

Challenge a Scarecrow - Scarecrows that guard a dangerous secret and a woman who believes she has brought her dog back to life add up to a frightening and deadly month for Jennet Ferguson. (#29)

Letter to Our Readers

Enjoy this book?

You can make a difference

As an independent publisher, Wings ePress, Inc. does not have the financial clout of the large New York Publishers. We can't afford large magazine spreads or subway posters to tell people about our quality books.

But, we do have something much more effective and powerful than ads. We have a large base of loyal readers.

Honest Reviews help bring the attention of new readers to our books.

If you enjoyed this book, we would appreciate it if you would spend a few minutes posting a review on the site where you purchased this book or on the Wings ePress, Inc. webpages at: https://wingsepress. com/

Thank You very much.

Visit Our Website

For The Full Inventory
Of Quality Books:

Wings ePress.Inc
https://wingsepress.com/

Quality trade paperbacks and downloads
in multiple formats,
in genres ranging from light romantic comedy
to general fiction and horror.
Wings has something for every reader's taste.
Visit the website, then bookmark it.
We add new titles each month!

Wings ePress Inc.

3000 N. Rock Road

Newton, KS 67114